Glimpses of Glory

Santosh Shailja

Ocean Paperbacks

A Division of Ocean Books Pvt. Ltd.

ISO 9001:2008 Publishers

Published by
Ocean Paperbacks
A Division of Ocean Books Pvt. Ltd.
4/19 Asaf Ali Road,
New Delhi-110 002 (INDIA)
e-mail: info@oceanbooks.in

ISBN 978-81-8430-169-4
Glimpses of Glory
by **Santosh Shailja**

Edition
First, 2012

Price
Rs. 150.00 (Rs. One Hundred Fifty only)

Printed at
Bhanu Printers, Delhi

Glimpses of Glory

Dedicated with
Reverence to
an ideal woman
Laxmi Bai Kelkar

Introduction

Each day dawns with a new sun. Every season brings new plants with new flowers and fruits. But each new plant has its close bond with mother-earth. Similarly with the change of time, new ideas, convictions and ideals are born in each century which mould human-lives. But the new is connected with the old just like a plant to its root. We Indians are blessed with a culture rich in lofty ideals and ideas which were nurtured by innumerable great men and women. History is full of such glorious sagas of life. No doubt, we remember them, worship too but never think of inculcating their ideals in our lives. This thought was at the back of my mind when I wrote this story book in Hindi named *Jauhar Ke Akhshar.* It was first published in 1966.

My friends and my daughter Renu exhorted me to translate these stories into English. This is my maiden attempt and I can only pray to God and hope for a kind and loving word from my readers. These short stories are about those great women (some girls too) who believed in great ideals of love, sacrifice, patriotism etc. and had the courage to live those ideals in their lives. They belong to different periods of history (some pre-historic) as well as different places and positions in society. I have not written their life history—it is just a glimpse into their life which shows their quality that proved them great and extraordinary. I do not present them as being super-human or heavenly bodies. They are just like any ordinary women but they achieved greatness by their commitment to their ideals. Therefore, readers will be surprised to read a new version of the story of Savitri or Parvati. But I believe that these great women need to be understood and emulated as our ideals. The new generation needs to know them in their true logical perspective. Otherwise we might forget them and their ideals in this age of materialism.

I again invoke your affection for my maiden attempt. But as a flow of the Ganges carries away everything—big or small—so I believe your affection would succeed in overlooking my verbal shortcomings and you will enjoy the contents of *Glimpses of Glory* as I have enjoyed every moment of rendering it into English.

My heartiest thanks to Shri Satish Dhar for his able support and assistance in bringing the book soon and in a presentable form. I am immensely grateful to the Publisher Shri Prabhat Kumar for his esteemed cooperation and support. My beloved husband Shri Shanta Kumar is always with me in each word that I have written so far, and my greatest inspiration comes from him.

Yamini Parisar
Palampur (H.P.)

—Santosh Shailja

Contents

Flower in Fire

Naana Sahib's Palace at Kanpur was besieged by giant cannons. British soldiers were ordered by General Auturam to blow it off. As Naana Sahib had escaped out of it, they plundered it to take revenge and now it was to be completely destroyed.

It was a grand palace which had entertained the English dignitaries too. It stood like a magnificent monument of wealth and glory. But how could the English tolerate it?

As the cannons were about to hit the Palace, a pretty girl of fourteen years came out of the Palace.

"Who are you? What are you doing here?" The in-charge asked in surprise.

The girl replied in English—"I am Maina and I am here to protect my palace."

"Maina? Naana Sahib's only daughter?" The commander was wonder-struck.

"Don't you remember me Sir? Your daughter was my dear friend?" She added with great confidence.

"Oh, yes, dear child: Now I recognise you well...Oh!" He was reminded of his dead daughter who had often visited Maina in her palace.

He held her hands affectionately, “What can I do for you? You must not stay here. Can I do anything for you dear?”

His sympathy brought tears in Maina’s eyes. She pleaded, “Yes, Sir, do help me if you can. I love my palace more than my life. Please, do not blow if off. Save my home from cannons...”

Her words and tears broke his heart. He could not refuse her. But how was he to disobey his supreme commander General Auturam?

He was in a fix...just then someone thundered from behind—“What’s going on here? Why is the palace not blown off yet?”

It was G. Auturam himself. The In-charge bowed and requested - “Sir, can’t this palace be left as it is?”

“No, never. You are an idiot. Blow it off immediately.”

The In-charge helplessly looked towards Maina...but she was nowhere. She must have slipped away when the General came.

After this, the cannons struck the palace like lightning. There was thunder and fire everywhere. In a few hours the beautiful palace was razed to the ground. Once a home of love and luxury was now a heap of bricks, full of dust and smoke.

After demolishing the palace, General Auturam was having a look around, when he heard someone weeping. He reached the corner and saw a girl sitting and weeping on a heap of burnt stones. In the moonlit night, she looked like a spirit of the palace mourning its death.

General recognised the girl and caught her—“where had you disappeared then? Why are you staying here? Why did not you go away with your father? Where is he now?” He bombarded her with questions.

But Maina did not reply and kept on weeping.

At this general lost his control and held her arm—“Hey, girl, answer me. Where is your father Naana?”

Now Maina got up and freeing her arm, spoke in anger, “I won’t reply any of your questions.”

General was cut to the quick. Her refusal sent him in a fit of rage - “How dare you refuse me an answer? Don’t you know the result?”

"I do know the result. But I am not afraid of you *firangis*. You are invaders. You have come to invade and loot our country."

The General could hear no longer. He ordered—"Arrest this...girl."

Maina was arrested and brought to Kanpur in police custody. She was questioned again and again and tortured to tell about her father's whereabouts. But that flower like girl had turned strong like a stone. Her lips were sealed. She proved to be the worthy daughter of her great father. No torture could waver her determination. At last the cruel British sentenced her to be burnt alive. This was the height of inhumanity—a girl of fourteen to be burnt alive. An only incident in the history of mankind! But she was as strong as the mountain. All-alone, surrounded by foreigners, she stood smiling in flames and opened her lips only to say—"*Jai Swaraj*."

□

The Youngest Martyr

"Long live revolution...long live *Tiranga* Flag..." with these slogans a procession of young revolutionaries was advancing to the police station. The leader was a 13 year old girl —Kanak Lata. The youngest revolutionary held the flag in her hand and challenged the British force with these words—"No one can dare to stop us from hoisting our flag now...." It was the year of 1942 and there was a national call from the freedom fighters to hoist the National Flag on the Police Chowki at Gohpur in Assam.

Kanak Lata's hands were small but their strength was great. Her body may be of a child but heart was of a warrior. Her words shot like fire-shells and the police rushed forward to stop their advance. But those small steps could not be stopped. So the police resorted to firing. First bullet pierced the young heart of Kanak Lata. 'Long live Kranti' with these words she gave the flag in someone's hands before falling down. The flag rose high from one hand to another...they did not let it fall on earth. One after another young sons and daughters of motherland sacrificed their lives to keep *Tiranga* flying. As they advanced towards the Chowki with the force of an Ocean, the policemen took to their heels.

This filled the atmosphere with shouts of victory.... The revolutionaries entered the Chowki like a Victorious army and hoisted the flag on the roof-top. All shouted with joy "*Jai Swaraj —Jai Kanak Lata* !"

□

Dedicated Flowers

While offering flowers and water to the holy *Tulsi*, she murmured: "O! Mother ! Your children are being tortured at the hands of foreigners...When would you save them?" Her throat was choked and eyes full of tears. Memories of cruelty by foreign masters flashed before her eyes...it was the year of 1897...Pune city was attacked by cholera. Mr. Reind was deputed as Officer-in-charge. His cruelty proved worse than cholera. As cholera raged in the city and people fell prey to it, Reind ruled mercilessly and punished people in the name of the dreaded disease. It was on his order that the policemen entered the homes with shoes on, desecrated idols in the worship-places and set them to fire, looted valuables, and molested women folk.... "Oh! Mother ! when will this dreaded dance of death stop...who will do it?"

"Maa.. We will do it." She heard these words and opened her eyes. There stood her sons Damodar and Balkrishan ! "You...? How will you do it?" She asked in her trembling voice.

Both took out pistols from their pockets and thundered.... "We will shoot that demon Reind and end his torture forever. Rest assured...mother."

"Rest assured..!" She repeated. How could she 'rest' when

two of her sons—one married and another in his teens, were ready to enter the jaws of death? She was even unable to imagine the result of this daring act. Even imagination made her heart tremble.

Damodar understood mother's dilemma and said, "Ma! can't you sacrifice your two sons for the sake of many sons and daughters of the land?"

Now she had no answer. With inhuman courage she blessed her sons—"May you succeed in you endeavour sons!"

As they touched her feet to go, she withheld her tears and prayed to Tulsi:—"Maiyya ! Bless them with success."

On that night when Mr. Reind and Mr. Amherst were returning from an official function, both were shot dead. Damodar and Balkrishan had kept their word. The news spread like wild fire. The people of Poona heaved a sigh of relief. Both brothers went into hiding. But the city had the worst taste of torture. There were arrests of innocent people. Armed With search warrants policemen entered the homes and took away men to torture in the police-custody. Some were put behind the bars. Even Lokmanya Bal Gangadhar Tilak was imprisoned for some days. The British police was groping in the dark. But as ill luck would have it, one greedy friend of Balkrishan was lured to give a clue to their hiding place. And police lost no time to capture Damodar. Balkrishan succeeded to escape to Hyderabad. Damodar surrendered and accepted that he had shot Mr. Reind to avenge his atrocities. He was sentenced to death. When one blossomed flower of mother was offered to motherland, how could the second one stay behind? Balkrishan returned to Pune and was immediately captured. But Government was unable to prove him guilty. So they called the younger brother Vasudev to give evidence against Balkrishan. At this proposal, Vasudev's conscience cried—"How can I give evidence against my patriotic brothers?"

He approached his mother – "Maa, I will go."

"Where, son ?" mother asked in apprehension.

"To same place...where your two brave sons have offered their lives, I, too, will follow them."

Mother was overwhelmed to hear the words of her third son. Her tear-bedimmed eyes were on him, who was just eighteen and ready to sacrifice his life for his motherland. Vasudev saw his mother's tears and said: "Ma...you offered your two flowers at the altar of motherland, won't you let the third one offer himself?"

She had no answer. She was torn between love and duty. She had to choose between the two and she chose duty. Wiping her tears, she spoke courageously "Go, my son, let motherland be blessed with your sacrifice."

With a smiling face Vasudev left home. He shot the traitors Ganesh Shankar and his brother, who had let down his brother and then surrendered in the court. He, too, was sentenced along with his elder brothers. All three flowers dedicated themselves at the altar of motherland.

□

Bhabhi

"Khat!...Khat...!!Khat...!!!" On hearing the knocking sound at the door, she hurried to open it. It was night and she was alone with her little son as her husband, revolutionary Bhagwaticharan, had gone underground due to his warrants in Meerut conspiracy case. On opening the door, she was surprised to see another revolutionary, Sukhdev, standing at the door. She could understand the urgency of his visit at this odd hour.

"Well, what brings you here at this moment?"

Sukhdev was quick to answer—"It is very urgent...Bhabhi, Can you travel out of the city tomorrow?"

"Where ? What for?" she asked cautiously.

"You know about Saunder's murder case. We have to help one of our revolutionary to get out of the town. If he stays in the city, he is sure to be caught by the police. You will have to pose as his wife and travel with him in a train."

"And what about my little son...Sachin?"

"Oh, Sachin will also travel with you and that will provide complete look of your family."

'Bhabhi Durga'—she was lovingly called by the revolutionary friends of her husband. She kept pondering over the situation.

She knew that Lala Lajpat Rai's death had been avenged by Bhagat Singh's shot and now the British Police was after his life. Chandershekhar Azad had made his escape out of Lahore city while Bhagat Singh's life was in danger. So he was to be sent out of the city safely. His precious life had to be saved at all cost. She decided in a moment. "Yes, I am ready to go."

Sukhdev's worried face brightened with joy. He explained the whole plan to her. Next morning they walked on the railway-platform as an up-to-date family of three—A clean-shaved, well-dressed *Sahib* in hat, his fashionably clad wife, with a chubby son followed by an attendant who was Sukhdev. They travelled in 1st class coach with great pomp and show. The boxes were inscribed in Roman letters—Captain J.J. They travelled out of Lahore city without any danger.

At Calcutta railway station, Bhagwati Charan had come to receive them. On seeing the family, Bhagawati Charan could not hide his surprise. He did not know—who were to be received. When he saw a clean-shaved Bhagat Singh, dressed in suit and hat like a sahib and his wife elegantly dressed with bright make-up, wearing high-heels, holding a fancy bag in one hand and little Sachin in the other—he smiled and whispered in her ear, "You gave the surprise of my life today. I salute to your spirit."

No doubt, Durga Bhabhi had an indomitable spirit of courage. She was ever ready to take any risk for the safety of her dear ones who were engaged in revolutionary movement against the British Raj. Bhagat Singh was one of her dearest brothers-in-law. She had a very soft corner for this young man who was the youngest in age and bravest of all.

But today while waiting for him in the Kudsia Garden in Delhi on April 8, 1929 she, her husband and son—all were very sad. Suddenly Sachin gave a cheerful cry - "Lamboo Chacha!" It was his favourite name for Bhagat Singh.

"Hello, Chhote Sabhib, how are you?" Bhagat Singh had started calling him this after their train journey together. Sachin was soon in his arms. Durga and Bhagwati got up and welcomed him with a smile. But today their smile was dimmed with sadness.

Bhagat singh looked at them and in his usual careless jolly voice spoke - “Why, Bhabhi, where are my Rasgullas and oranges? Have you forgotten to bring these?”

Forcing a smile Bhabhi took out both from his basket.” How could I forget your favourites? Now, have these and eat to your heart’s content today...because...tomorrow...?”

And she kept the rest in her heart as she knew that their won’t be any ‘tomorrow’ now. Only today they could see talk and enjoy Bhagat Singh’s company because he had been chosen to throw Bomb in the Assembly Hall and there was no hope of his returning alive from there.

At this thought Bhabhi let out a great sigh and her eyes were filled with tears. Bhagat Singh who was immersed in eating noted this and was quick to say : “No...No...Bhabhi these sighs and tears are not worthy of you...not fit for the gallant Bhabhi of Bhagat Singh...And who knows the future? You might again have to play the part of that fashionable Mem Sahib to this Sahib?” And this made everyone burst into laughter.

Bhabhi wiped her tears and tried to smile but her heart could not reconcile with this cruel fact that her dear brother-in-law would be no more coming to her with his endearing address ‘Bhabhi.’ Then she heard him saying good-bye. “...Well...Bhabhi...allow me to take leave now—be always happy...Vande Matram!”

□

The Revolutionary

"Mother, today I shall go to the University." Veena said excitedly.

"Yes, I know, today you are to receive your Degree in Honours." Mother replied happily.

"But I shall not accept the Degree."

"Why?" Mother asked with surprise. Veena did not reply. Mother watched her daughter. She knew her daughter's mind. She remembered her elder daughter, too, had refused to accept degree like her. Then, she had left studies and joined the freedom struggle. Was Veena, too, following her sister's footsteps?

Those were the days of *Bang-Bhang* movement. Each and every youth of Bengal was active in revolutionary activities. There was only one aim of every young girl or boy—to possess a revolver and shoot down the British ruler.

Kalyani and Veena Das were two daughters of eminent educationist Veni Madhav Das. He was a staunch patriot who had contact with Netaji Subash Chander Bose. Kalyani had taken active part in the agitation when Simon Commission visited India. She was arrested and tortured in the prison. Veena was seething with anger and was determined to avenge her sister.

She got the opportunity on 6th Feb, 1922 at the Convocation Function of Calcutta University. The Viceroy of Bengal was to preside over the function. As soon as Mr. Jackson got up to award the degree to the student, Veena Das drew out her revolver and shot at him thrice. But unfortunately, she missed the target and he escaped while his companion Dr. Dinesh Chander was wounded.

Soon there was a great hue and cry in the hall. Veena attempted again but failed. Next moment she was caught by the policemen. She was only twenty one years old. In prison-cell she was given inhuman torture. She was forced to tell the names and addresses of the other revolutionaries. But they failed to elicit any information from that girl of iron will. At last a special Tribunal was appointed under Bengal Criminal Law Amendment Act to convict her. On that day the whole of calcutta attended the court to see and hear her. Veena stood in court with her head held high. There was no trace of fear or remorse on her smiling face. In a loud and bold voice she thundered—"Yes, I shot at the Governor because I deem it as my duty to punish the British who have enslaved our motherland. I have no sorrow or fear for this act—rather I feel proud to do my duty."

Veena was awarded rigorous imprisonment by the British court. But her indomitable spirit could not be crushed. She lived long to become the vice-principal of a college when the British left India in 1947.

□

Architect of National Flag

An Indian house in London was hosting a farewell party for Madam Cama who had come there for an operation. After the successful operation, she was leaving for India. Amidst pleasant talk, one of her friends said, "Now you will have to be very careful for your health. You know, all that hectic political activity cost you this health problem."

On her advice Madame Cama smiled, "I will remember your words. But you, too, know that I cannot remain indoors just confined to myself. I cannot live without work."

At this, a young man came to her side—"Madam, I want to have a word with you. I am Shyam Krishan Verma..."

Interrupting him, Madam Cama spoke—"Yes, I have heard much about the great revolutionary Shyamji and I feel happy to meet you."

Shyamji spoke to her in a low voice, "Madam, I have come with a special request for you. If you want to work for your country, do not go back to India. While staying here you can work more and do a lot for the organisation I beseech you to lead the revolutionary activities here."

Madam Cama, who was a revolutionary at heart and a great worker, understood Shyamji's words. She took instant decision and cancelled her journey. That farewell party turned into her welcome party for the revolutionary movement in London. She was already engaged in freedom movement in India. She had worked with many organisations and participated in Indian National Congress movement too.

Madam Cama addressed a public meeting at the famous Hyde Park in London. In a fiery speech she spoke about the inhuman British rule in India. She exhorted Indians to plunge themselves heart and soul into this struggle for freedom. The public was impressed with her words—"Freedom is our birth right and the British have no right to deprive us from this." Thus, she justified all revolutionary activities. The people were surprised at her courage to challenge the British in England. But the Government could not let it go on. Her speeches, pamphlets had created a great stir in London. Government threatened her with a warning of deportation from England.

But Madam Cama proved faster in her move. She escaped into France through the British Channel. The British Government did not allow her to enter England or India for thirty five years. But this could not deter her from her path. Her voice could not be silenced. She carried on with her speeches and writings. 'Vande Matram' was a magazine which ran successfully due to her efforts. She met and inspired many revolutionaries like Lala Hardayal, Acharaya Virender, Veer Savarkar and Chattopadhayay. In fact, she proved to be a forceful crusader for the freedom movement outside India.

In a conference of World Socialist Meet at Stuttgart in Germany, she represented India amid representatives of many other countries.

Her impressive speech drew praise and respect from all. She presented the case for India's freedom in such a way that all supported her cause. In the end, she showed extraordinary courage to hoist her country's future flag *Tiranga* on stage. Everyone saluted the flag and applauded her. It was the first time that *Tiranga* was unfurled out of India before it was hoisted in free India on 15th Aug. 1947.

□

A Martyr's Mother

At the gate of Gorakhpur Prison, Kakori case convict Ram Prasad Bismil's father was surprised to see his wife. He did not want to bring her along because he knew that a mother could not bear her dear son to be sentenced to death. So he came alone to see his revolutionary son for the last meeting. But here she was bravely standing at the prison door. As both stepped forward, a young man darted forth—"Mataji, please, take me along with you."

"Who are you and why do you want to accompany us ?" She looked at his face.

"I am Shiv Verma and Bismilji is not only my companion but my inspiration also. I must pay last regards to my Guru and ask him certain confidential facts."

Mother understood his sincerity and replied, "Come along my son, don't be afraid of anyone. If they ask your identity, tell them that you're our nephew. Rest assured, I will take care of everything."

Mother's boldness surprised not only the youth but her husband too. Because day before he had refused this youth to take along because of the police.

All of them reached near Bismil's cell. He came forward, said Pranam to father, Namaste to his companion. But when he looked towards his mother, he could utter no words...his heart became heavy and he burst into tears.

Mother stood calm and quiet. After a while she spoke in her affectionate tone—"Dear Ram, why do you shed tears? I know you are my brave son—whose name is enough to make the British police tremble at heart. You are not the one who should be afraid of death. I have not come here to sympathise or condole my son's sentence. No, I have come to congratulate my brave son. I thought myself as the luckiest mother to have a son like you, but your tears make me ashamed. Son, if you were so scared of this sentence, why had you taken the vow of revolution?" Everyone was stunned to listen to her words. Prison-officer spoke out – "Only such a brave mother gives birth to a son like this."

Bismil controlled himself and wiped his tears. Now he remembered how his mother had always supported and helped him in his revolutionary activities. Sometimes when his father and grand-mother opposed him, it was only his mother's support that helped him with money and encouraging words. He was overwhelmed with respect and bowed to her – "Maa...I am blessed to be your son. These tears were not born out of fear of death...I felt sad for you – for my inability to serve you and leave you alone. I feel sorry for you...Maa !"

Mother put her loving hand on his shoulder through the bars and spoke with love – "No, dear son, do not feel sorry for us. To be your mother – a martyr's mother – is enough to keep me blessed for my whole life."

And she proved true to her words. She never felt sorry or wavered in courage – not when poverty struck the family and another son died due to lack of treatment. Then her husband, too, left her alone in the world. Her young daughter committed suicide. The elder one became a widow. Braving all these calamities, that martyr's mother never shook her faith and always lived these words of her son Bismil–

"Maalik Teri Raza Rahe, Aur tu hi tu rahe
Bakki na men rahun, na meri arju rahe."

□

Life-Partner

The iron-gate of the Prison House screeched to open. A young lady entered and rushed towards the prison-cell with a sentry. With a trembling heart and tear-bedimmed eyes she looked into the dark cell. There was a movement in darkness and the prisoner came to stand before her.

They stood facing each-other – husband and wife Balmukund and Ramrakhi. He belonged to a patriotic family of martyrs Bhai Permanand and Bhai Matidas. He was one of the youths who dared to throw a bomb on a convoy of Viceroy Lord Hardinge at Delhi on Dec. 23, 1912. He was captured along with thirteen youths. There was a drama of court proceedings for seven days and then they were sentenced to death.

The news – 'To be hanged' reached his newly wedded wife while she was still in her parents' home. It was only one year since they were married and she was to leave for her husband's home first time to live as his wife. This devastating news was like a bolt from the blue. Her life was shattered before beginning. She rushed straight to meet her husband.

"What are you thinking? Are you afraid of my sentence?" His question brought her back from her thoughts.

Forcing a smile, she replied – “No, I am not afraid...I will never forbid you to sacrifice your life for the country but...

“Why but?” he asked.

“But why did you choose to tread this path without me? I am your partner in life as well as in death too.” Her words made him speechless. He was overwhelmed with joy and pride in his brave wife.

After a while, she asked, “What do you eat here?”

“This dry bread made of sand and dust” he showed a crumb of Roti.

“And where do you sleep?”

He pointed towards a dark corner full of mosquitoes – “There, with two blankets.” As she saw and heard everything, her heart broke with unbearable pain. With heavy heart she bade him farewell and returned.

After reaching home she dug a hole in her room just like that in the prison-cell...she made it damp with water. She discarded her fine clothes and jewellery. She wore coarse clothes and prepared her bread out of dough mixed with sand. She started living a hard life as in prison-cell. She denied everything which was denied to her husband.

On the appointed day of his death, she got up early in the morning, dressed herself like a bride and thinking of her dear husband sat down with eyes closed. As he was hanged to death in the prison, she breathed her last at home. Both were put on one pyre and consigned to flames together. She had vowed to be with him for ever. How could death take him alone?

□

A Pillar of Strength

A village woman was walking slowly on the Kosma station. She was accompanied by a young man. She could put one foot after the other with great effort. It looked as if she was suffering from an attack of joint pains. After reaching the destination, both stayed at an inn. When inside, she removed two big guns which were tied to her legs.

She was Shastri, sister of great revolutionary of Kakori case Ram Prasad Bismil who used to travel along with his sister to carry guns, revolvers etc for use in revolutionary activities. Her courage and intelligence was the greatest asset for his brother. She dressed in loose clothes of kurti-lehanga which successfully hid guns and revolvers. A big dupatta encircled her upper body. This served her brother's purpose and he was always grateful to his sister. Many times he was saved from being caught by the police due to her presence of mind.

But one day Shastri's wit failed her and police over-powered Ram Prasad Bismil from his home. Before leaving, Ram Prasad touched his parents' feet and embraced her sister. He said, "Dear sister, you have always been at my side and now I entrust you with our parents to take care while I am away. You have always been my pillar of strength."

Sister bid a tearful good-bye to her brother. She knew at heart that they won't be able to meet again. Ram Prasad was charged with many offences and sentenced to death. She remained like a pillar of strength for her parents. Misfortunes never come alone. So she lost her husband too. But she forgot her own grief and served her parents. The family suffered from acute poverty. So one of her brother-died of disease while a sister committed suicide. After sometime, father, too died of shock. But Shastri never lost her courage. With great patience she looked after her mother and son. She was an uneducated village woman but her qualities of patience, courage and wisdom were no less than great revolutionary Ram Prasad Bismil, for whom she was a real 'pillar of strength.' Her sacrifice is not known in the history of freedom struggle. But she served like a foundation stone of Mother India's Temple.

□

A Shattered Dream

S*here-Punjab* Raja Ranjit Singh's dead body was consigned to flames. His wife Rani Jinda stood holding her young son's hand. Gazing at the flames she vowed to her departed husband – "I will fulfil your dream. No *Firangi* would ever dare touch your beloved Punjab."

Fire of the pyre now burnt in Rani Jinda's heart. She was determined to rule over her state with the same zeal of patriotism. She had an indomitable spirit of a lioness.

But as ill luck would have it, the Sikhs suffered a humiliating defeat at the enemy's hands in the battle of 1845. When Senapati Hari Singh broke the news to Rani Jinda – "Maharani ji, we have lost our Punjab to the British. Now you are dethroned and left with only a pension of Rs.1.50 lac."

The news was like a bolt from the blue. Rani saw her dream shattered. Her words spoke of her immense sorrow, "Now, what will become of my dear Punjab?"

But she did not lose heart. She did not accept defeat and started preparation for another battle. Using the pension-fund, she raised an army and bought ammunitions. The British Government came to know of this and cut short her pension to Rs. 40,000 only. Even this could not deter Rani from her struggle for freedom. She carried on her preparations with a stronger zeal. But the Govt. overpowered her and sent her to Banaras Jail.

Rani stood behind the bars like a lioness in iron-cage. Her dear husband dead, state snatched and her son sent away to England by the British. She had nothing except her courage and strong will to fight for freedom. Holding her dagger tightly, she vowed again "I won't accept defeat. A lioness can never be kept in a cage."

And she proved to be a true lioness. She disguised herself as a Nun and deceiving the policemen escaped from Jail. Now she journeyed towards Nepal. She received a Royal welcome in Nepal and asylum to live in peace. But her soul craved for freedom from the British ruler. She could not forget for a moment that her Punjab was enslaved.

Now the only hope was her own son Dilip who was studying in England. She planned to go to England and be with her son. She dreamt of leading the army with her son as the leader. She imagined to see him like his illustrious father Ranjit Singh – the Lion of Punjab.

Rani Jinda took a long and hard journey to England. Throughout journey, she kept on making plans of raising a new army to challenge the British in Punjab. Her hopes soared high. She had deep faith and iron will to turn her dream into a reality. Her ship touched the shores of England but her hopes were dashed to the ground when she saw her son. There stood Dilip Singh who was her son only in name – dressed like an Englishman-speaking English – no trace of the legacy of his great father. Within a few days she realised that not only his exterior but interior, too, had turned English. He was promised the Title of Raja under the British rule and he was happy in that luxurious life. Without self-respect and love of the country he had become a puppet in the hands of the British rulers. Rani felt suffocated in this atmosphere. Her heart broke. Her courage failed. Dark future of slavery threatened her free spirit. She had taken a vow to fight against slavery. But her son was the last setback to her plans.

With no hope from her son she lost the will to live. She died heart-broken. Away from her dear Punjab, she died in England. Her free spirit flew away to the land of her dreams.

□

Spirit of Revolution

When the British Residents Parson and Emerson reached Mandi State, they were shocked at the hostile attitude of the public. The Himalayan people did not welcome them with the usual warmth; rather they expressed their protest. The easy way with which Kullu state had been annexed by the clever British did not seem to work here. What was the reason? Who was the inspiration behind this revolutionary atmosphere? Who had put fire in the cool docile eyes of simple hilly people? It was due to the Rani of Khergadhi – though widowed and issueless, she was leading the revolution like the Rani of Jhansi.

The Rani had prepared everything for the Day of Revolt. But one problem worried her. There was none who knew the art of bomb-making. One day a young revolutionary from Lahore approached her with the solution. Rani's eyes shone with happiness – "Now none can stop us in our revolutionary march." After this, the preparations got a new lease of life. Rani gave up her royal distance and mingled freely with people. She encouraged and employed the common people into her army. The revolutionary army was being raised out of these patriotic youth. Rani's courage and patriotism was electrifying the people to fight for freedom of their State.

The British rulers could not annex the State in their usual way because Rani outsmarted them by making Yoginder Sen the Crown Prince while she had the reins of the state in her hands. The rulers were helplessly watching the Rani strengthening her force.

But misfortune befell her soon. As Rani sat in her palace, planning her future, a young man came running –"Rani Sahiba, we are lost – the British got a clue of our revolutionary Wing and they have captured many persons in the State. Bhai Hridaya Ram, Bhai Hardev Ram too have been arrested."

On hearing this devastating news, Rani was stunned. Extreme sorrow brought tears into her eyes. Her strong fort of Revolution was dazed to the ground.. The enemy had crushed the movement before it could rise – But how could they get the clue?

Suddenly she asked – "And is the In-charge of that Wing safe?" Before he could reply, the police entered – "Rani Sahiba, here is a warrant for you." Now she knew the answer. It was due to the betrayal of that In-charge which brought this misfortune at her doorstep.

The Rani was charged with treason and sentenced for life imprisonment in Lucknow prison. When that fiery *Spirit of Revolution* was being taken away from her Hill state, even the mountains were moved to tears.

□

Vow for Freedom

Belhongal Fort of Kittur in Mysore State was enveloped in darkness. It was pitch dark inside a cell of the Prison. But standing behind the bars, her eyes shone like pools of fire. She was Rani Chenamma of Kittur who was imprisoned there after she lost a battle against the British army.

As she gazed at her fort, tears blinded her eyes and she muttered with grief – "Ah! My dear Kittur! Both of us are unfortunate – enslaved by the enemy – helpless – "

Images of bygone days flashed before her eyes. It seemed like yesterday only when they lived a blissful life in the sunshine of her husband Raja Mallsaraj Desai. But darkness clouded her sun when the king was snatched by death. She took heart and enthroned her son. She took the reigns of the state in her able hands. But destiny willed otherwise. Her son, too, was snatched by the cruel hands of death. Rani felt shattered and alone. But like a true mother of her people, she forgot her own grief and plunged into work.

But another misfortune waited for her in the garb of the British. Rani knew that the *Firangi* ruler was waiting for an opportunity to annex the State. And two greedy ministers' treachery provided the opportunity. Everything happened suddenly and Rani was shocked to see the enemy knocking at the gate of the fort. She steeled herself against the misfortune and decided to fight back.

The British General Thenkarey offered her to surrender and get back her crown. But Rani thundered like a lioness.... "Kittur's Crown is not at the mercy of the *Firangis.* We will fight and win it."

A fierce battle was fought between the British and Rani Chennama. Rani's army fought with a will 'to do or die'. The Rani herself was with them at every front. So she inflicted a humiliating defeat at the enemy with General Thenkarey's head as a prize. The rejoicing over the victory made people wild with joy.

But Rani did not loosen her grip because she knew her path was beset with thorns. Now the Fort In-charge played into the enemy's hands. Treachery hit Rani again and there was a second attack from the British. This time the enemy proved stronger. The Rani planned to leave the Fort and attack the enemy with outside help. But she was captured while trying to get out of the Fort.

Rani was put behind the bars and a reign of terror was let loose on the public.

"But this prison cannot keep me long. I will get out and fight back with Rayanna's soldiers." Rani muttered while holding the iron-bars. Her eyes shone with new hope. She had secret information of his Sipasalar Rayanna's Gorilla warfare. She had encouraging news of his brave soldiers' rising strength. One day Rayanamma came to meet her in a disguise and whispered excitedly, "Ranima! Rest assured, we have raised a powerful army with enough arms. Our victory march has travelled through Nandgarh, Someshwergarh, Pratapgarh and Khanapur. Our last victory will be at Haliyal and that would complete the victory of Kittur."

"Victory of Kittur" – these words felt like nectar to the dying soul of Rani. She gave away all ornaments in Rayanna's hands and said, "Now all my hopes rest with you. You will succeed and free our beloved Kittur. I have full faith in you."

** ** ** ** ** **

The dawn was about to break. The night was giving way to day. Rani Chenamma welcomed the rays of the rising sun. Her eye were full of hope for free Kittur.

"Rani Sahiba," Prison officer Harris's voice shattered her dream. "A very bad and sad news.... The British have captured Rayanna with his men...and hanged all to death and..." he stopped as if unable to tell the rest.

"And...?" Rani asked with a sinking heart.

"And your daughter-in-law killed her son and herself too."

As he uttered the last word, Rani fell down like a fallen tree...muttering "Everyone left...my last hope Rayanna, and crown-Prince too...now Chenamma also leaves you dear Kittur...but with a vow to be born again to make you free."

□

Ma Sharda

A small group of pilgrims was going from Jai Ram Baro village to Calcutta for a holy dip in the Ganges river. An eighteen year old girl, too, accompanied them. She was called Sharda. Her Young face showed more anxiety than excitement. She was married and it was her first visit to her husband. She was only seven when her parents got her married. Then she did not know what marriage meant. When she was fourteen, she was sent to her husband's house for the first time. She was totally new not only to the place but its people and other mundane duties. But her husband was patient enough to teach her each and everything. She had faint memories of those days. But her stay was not long. She came back after a fortnight and four years went by but her husband never called her back. She knew he worked as a priest in Dakhineshwar Temple near Calcutta. There were rumours that he never took care of himself and lived like a monk. Sharda's heart was pained to hear this. She felt deep love and regard for him and wanted to look after him. So, she decided to accompany those pilgrims and reach Calcutta to be with her husband. Calcutta was 80 miles away. Her father accompanied her. Journey was hard and long. She had to walk all the way. Due to exhaustion, fever gripped her body.

When she reached Dakhineshwar Temple – the abode of her husband Ram Krishan, cool and holy atmosphere of the temple felt like balm to her suffering body. On seeing them, Ram Krishan was too surprised to speak. He touched his father-in-law's feet and took them inside. His heart went out to see her suffering. But Sharda's heart rejoiced to be with her husband. This happiness proved a panacea for all her ills. Fever left her and she settled happily in the home.

But days went by and her husband did not meet her. She cleaned, cooked and did everything as the housewife but could not see him. "Has he forgotten that he is married and his wife waits for him day and night?" Sharda kept thinking with a heavy heart. One evening Ram Krishan sent for her. She entered his room and sat at his feet. While pressing his feet, she gave vent to her feelings – "What do you think of me?" this was a question from a lonely wife to her husband.

But Ram Krishan's reply stunned her. He said, "I regard you just like the mother sitting in that Devi temple – a mother who gave me birth and is now pressing my feet like her son."

Sharda was struck dumb. She could not understand first and when she understood their deep meaning, she felt numb with sorrow. Her whole world stood shattered – all her dreams of happy married life were finished in a moment. She looked into his eyes. There was a look of childlike love and faith in his eyes. That look transformed her completely. Sharda forgot that she was a wife to him. Her whole self underwent a change and in that moment she felt herself as he had called her "Mother!"

She got up, put away her veil and touched his feet calling him – "Gurudev !"

On that day a new Sharda was born who was not his wife but his disciple as any other one. She started living life like his other disciples. But Ram Krishan tested her and told her to share his bed for eight months. And Sharda proved true to his faith and strength of character. She lived with him as a mother with her son. This filled Ram Krishan's heart with immense bliss. He bowed before her and spoke – "If you had not been so pure and desireless, how could I remain pure on my path to God?"

That simple, uneducated girl who was born in a village, rose to a great height in Ram Krishan's spiritual life. She cooked and cared for all who came to meet Ram Krishan. She was not only a mother but an inspiration to all who took Sanayas with Vivekanand. When Ram Krishan died after prolonged illness, she remained true to her duty as mother and Guru to all. Ram Krishna had told her – "Never think yourself alone – I will be always with you. So do not dress like a widow – you will be Suhagin for ever." So Sharda Mother never wore a widow's white sari without border. She remained as the blessed mother in true sense.

□

Nanda Deep

There was a mammoth gathering in a hall at London. Thousand eyes were riveted to that young Indian monk – Swami Vivekananda. Everyone present there was mesmerised by his words At last, the fervent orator ended his speech with these words: "If I could get only twenty dedicated persons with me, I would change the face of the world." A spell fell on the audience as if a lightning had struck.

Next day a young lady came to Vivekananda's residence.

"What brings you here, Devi?" He asked.

"You asked for twenty dedicated persons, I have come to offer myself as one of them." She replied in a sweet but strong voice.

Vivekananda looked at her with eyes full of affection and appreciation. There stood an English girl tall, beautiful and devoted. Her eyes shone with intelligence and determination. She was Miss Margaret Nobel—born in Ireland to Christian parents. Her father was a bishop. She was educated in London. From her early days she was attracted towards spiritualism and Indian Vedanta. When she had a chance to listen to Vivekanand's discourses in London, her attraction turned into love and faith.

On hearing his call, she made up her mind to dedicate her life towards this goal. She had realised that she belonged to Bharat and its Vedanta. She desired to go to India to see its each nook and corner and to know its spiritual treasure. One day she asked: "Swamiji, How can I best serve India?"

"By becoming one with India." Vivekananda's reply was an indication of her future line of action.

She reached India in Jan., 1898. Swami Vivekananda sent her to live with guru Ma Sharda—wife of RamKrishna ParamHansa. Margarete started living with Ma Sharda like an Indian daughter. She toured India with Vivekananda and understood Indian culture and its life. As she came into contact of Indians, she noticed two anomalies in Indian society. The lofty ideals of religion and the lowest society caught in superstitions, illiteracy and poverty. She felt sorry for this and was anxious to do a lot to improve this.

At last the day of Initiation arrived—she had waited long for it. Her Guru Vivekananda initiated her with this gospel, "May you possess the heart of a mother, will-power of a warrior, sweetness of air, devotion of the lamp. May you be India's daughter, servant, friend – everything." He blessed her with a new name Bhagini Nivedita (Sister Nivedita). She was the first and foremost initiated woman into Hindu Dharma.

"The dedication of the lamp" became her life's basic Mantra. She plunged herself body and soul into the uplift of Indian society.

Educational Institution was her first contribution to the Indian women. She noticed that Indian girls were not permitted to go out of the boundary of homes to get education. She had to struggle a lot for this. When she opened first Girls school in Calcutta, there were very few students. After days of meeting and persuading Indian mothers, she was able to get students admitted in her school. But she had full support from Sharda Ma. And this 'Nivedita Balika Vidalaya' proved to be the first milestone in educating Indian girls. But her concept of education was of Gurukula tradition. She did not want the girls to become 'Mem Sahiba' immersed in Western culture rather her aim was to make them truly Indian. She said - "I want you to emulate the ideals of Sita, Savitiri,

Laxmibai, Rani Padmini, Ahlaya Bai etc. in your lives."

When Rabindra Nath Tagore sent his daughter to her to learn Western culture and etiquettes Nivedita was quick to remark – "Why are you bent upon turning her into an English lady (Memsahiba.) She is an Indian girl. Let her learn her own Bangali Language and Indian culture."

Nivedita had great respect for the scientist Jagdish Chander Bose who was the first to discover the Theory of Life in Plants. But she was pained to see that the scientist could not get the fame and support to pursue his discovery because he was a citizen of a poor and slave country. So she decided to extend him a helping hand. She helped Bose in editing, printing and publishing his books and getting him recognition in England. She also worked hard to construct Bose Laboratory to further his experiments.

Those were the days of Bang-Bhang Movement when Bengal was undergoing through a revolutionary agitation; she felt the need of an able leader who should channelize this agitation. She approached Arvindoo Ghosh who was a prominent learned man of that time. She told him, "Arvindo Babu! you are not made to be just a teacher in a college. You have the talent to teach and lead the society. Your country needs you now. Bengal is calling you."

"But I need companions to work with me." Arvindo said. At this, Nivedita's reply was – "You can have me as your first companion." After that she plunged into this agitation with Arvindoo Ghosh. Her words were great inspiration for Bangali youth – "Attack your enemy with full force, have a blood-bath; this is the only way to freedom." This enlightened lady was an inspiration to scientist Prafull Chander Rai, Historian Yadu Nath Sarkar, Radha Kumud Mukerji, Veer Savarkar, Gopal Krishan Gokhale, Ras Bihari Bose, Bipin Chander Pal, Madame Cama and Shyamji Krishan Verma etc. She was like a Nandadeep which lights many other *deeps*.

At last she succumbed to hard work and fell seriously ill. In her last days she was with Amla Bose, wife of Sir Jagdish Chander Bose at Darjeeling. It was the morning of 13th Oct. 1911. Nivedita was lying in the lap of her dear Bhabhi. Memories of her past days flashed before her eyes. First memory was of her parents in Ireland when she was just an innocent small girl. She could remember his father's last words to her mother – "Look, we have dedicated our daughter for God's work. If and when His call comes, do not forbid her from her mission in life." Her mother always remembered these words. So when her daughter asked for her permission to go to India forever, she blessed her with her consent.

The second memory was of her Guru Swami Vivekananda when he initiated her before a holy fire lit in the Ashram courtyard at Dakhinesewar Temple in Calcutta. His words rang in her ears – "Nivedita, May you imbibe the dedication of the Lamp in your life." As she breathed her last, she had the smile of fulfilment on her lips.

□

Daughter of India

Madan Mohan Malviya – the great nationalist,educationist - was sitting with a worried face when a European lady visited him. She, too, was an eminent educationist - Mrs.Annie Besant who had opened a college to educate students about Hindu culture. Malviyaji had great respect for her.

Mrs. Besant noticed Malviya's worried look. "Sir, you look upset today. What is troubling you? Can I help in any way?"

Her sympathy moved Malviyaji's heart. He replied "Yes, I am troubled with a problem. I had long cherished the dream of opening a Hindu University in Banaras. But I have not been able to collect enough funds for it. There is no hope of my dream to become a reality."

Mrs. Besant thought for a while. Her face shone with a determination and she said "Mahamana, don't be disheartened. Your dream will become a reality. I will help you."

Malviyaji tried to smile – "Mrs Besant, I heartily thank you for your kind words. But how much can you help to build a University?"

Mrs. Besant smiled and said, "Sir, I do not offer funds, I offer you my Central Hindu College to make it your Banaras Hindu University."

Malviyaji was too surprised to speak. He could not believe his ears—" But how could you give away your college which is the product of your hard work and wealth."

"Mahamana! This college is not my personal property. It belongs to the nation. And I offer it to you to make it a University to serve a greater purpose for the Hindu students. Who else would be a better trustee of my college than your good self?"

Mahamana Malviyaji was overwhelmed with joy. His life's dream 'Banaras Hindu University' was becoming real due to Mrs. Besant's unprecedented sacrifice. When she took leave of him, he had tears of joy and gratitude for that European Lady who loved India more than any Indian.

Though born in Ireland, Annie Besant had adopted India as her motherland when she came here on 16th Nov. 1893. While in England, she had been a member of the Theosophical Society and studied Vedanta and Hindu scriptures. When she came to India, she was shocked to see the inhuman British rule. She was also pained to see the sufferings of people from poverty, illiteracy and superstitions.

Ms. Annie Besant made up her mind to revive the old Vedic values in Hindu youth through education. She was the best orator of her time. Her famous words are – "Bharat and Hinduism are inseparable – The day India relinquishes her Hinduism, India would be nowhere." She thought and spoke like a Hindu Rishi (thinker). To educate the youth in a nationalist way, she opened the Central Hindu College. This institution attracted all nationalists and educationalists. It became the hub of freedom activists too. And when Mrs. Besant gave the institution to Mahamana Madan Mohan Malviya, it proved a milestone in the history.

Mrs. Besant was deeply anguished to see India under British slavery. When England was engaged in First World War, Annie Besant gave a call to Indian youth – "Now is the golden opportunity to strike at the British rulers." Her courage surprised all. She was honoured by being made the President of Indian National Congress. Mrs. Besant gave active support in establishing Home Rule League,

National Convention and Commonwealth of India League. The British rulers tried to stop her activities and put her in prison. But she could not be silenced. After her release, she was again, up in arms against the British rule. This forced Mr. Montegew to visit India and announce some important reformatory acts.

After devoting forty years of valuable service for India, this illustrious daughter breathed her last in this land.

□

Lost Light

A frosty evening at Bedenviler in Germany in 1936. An Indian youth was walking rapidly to a Nursing Home. His handsome face was distorted with worries. His pained look travelled from snow-clad earth to misty sky but could find no ray of hope anywhere. At last he reached the Nursing Home. His heart was heavy with sadness and even in this cold weather there was sweat on his brow.

"Kamala...aa...!" His heart-rending voice touched her ears and she opened her eyes – there he was...her dear husband Jawahar Lal Nehru !

"You...you have come to me...when, and how...?" It was an unexpected pleasant surprise for her . She could never ask for more than this . He had been in prison for taking part in Freedom-movement, while his wife was brought to this nursing home due to serious illness.

He gazed at her withered face and took her hand in his hands and said: "Yes, I have come to you and now you will be all right soon..."

Kamala's face brightened up with hope and eyes were filled with light. But after a while she asked, "But you were in Almora prison? Then, how could you come here? Did you ask for..." She could not complete her question but her husband understood her apprehension. He held her hands and spoke with emotion - " No, my dear, you are afraid that your husband might had been forced to ask for 'pardon' to reach you. No, darling, how could your brave husband be so coward? It is the British Govt. who asked me to look after you here for some days."

At this, Kamala heaved a sigh of relief and smiled sweetly. Now with her dear husband at her side, she experienced immense relief from pain...mental as well as physical. Her health started improving. There was hope everywhere. Even doctors noticed this change in her condition. Every morning brought a new sun as it brought her husband along. And every evening turned sunny as she was not alone. Jawahar brought her flowers and sat besides her narrating his experiences and incidents which filled her lonely hours. She began talking and laughing with him. In these secluded moments both enjoyed a real honeymoon of their married life. They had been married for twenty years. It seemed just yesterday that Jawahar was married to this sweet pretty bride from Kashmir. She was too shy to ask for anything. She knew she was married to a person who was not only a dear husband but a devoted son of the soil, who had to be out in freedom-movement. So she reconciled with his absence and never put any obstacle in his activities. Her calm and courageous words were, "If you are engaged in daring acts for the country, I won't let you down...I am always with you."

And she proved this once when he was in Naini prison. Kamala led the movement in Allahabad. Her leadership qualities came to be recognised by all at that time. She was popular among all women...rich or poor. Even her father-in-law Motilal Nehru praised her for this. "How could such a shy and soft girl turn into a rock of strength and determination?" Jawahar wondered while looking at her now.

But this took a toll on her and her health started deteriorating. Those long spells of loneliness and struggle had an adverse effect on her sensitive body. She became so sick that she had to be admitted to this nursing home in Lausanne at the end of 1936 in Germany. It was the best for her health. But Jawahar could not be with her.

And now his presence had filled her days with hope and joy.

"I have never been so happy ever...I feel blessed as never before..." While Kamala spoke these words...Jawahar nodded...." Yes, of course...." But Kamala sensed his absent mindedness.

"What's the matter? You are not mentally present here at this moment. Where are you?"

"Yes, I was not here....I was thinking of the Annual Convention of Congress party which has proposed me to preside on it. But how can I go now?. No, I shall Say 'No' and remain with you here."

On hearing this, Kamala's heart missed a beat. Her face was drained of colour. Jawahar saw this. He immediately held her hand..."No Kamala dear, I am not leaving you...Never. I will be with you here...Let them have the convention. Someone else would preside...how can I go...no...no..."

Kamala understood his dilemma. It was a choice between his wife and his country...She decided not to come between the two. As she had always done....She mustered all her courage and tried to smile. "No, you cannot say 'No' to your work. Your country needs you...do not be worried for me. You know I am better now. I promise to remain like this. You must go."

It was the night of 27th February. Jawahar was at her bed-side. Holding her hands, he again asked, "Kamala, do you promise to be well and waiting for me when I go tomorrow?"

"Yes, yes, yes" she tried to laugh..."Should I write this on a Stamp-paper?" At this Jawahar felt reassured.

He stayed there for the night. Little daughter Indira was also with him. At the last hour of night, Kamala gave a piteous cry..."Look...who is there...calling me?" Jawahar rushed to her side...doctors, too, came running. Little daughter began to cry...Jawahar touched her forehead and spoke in a choked voice– "Kamala...look towards me...I am here...your daughter is here. There is no one else...look to me." his words were frozen on his lips...Kamala was no more. The light was lost...and there was only darkness for him. In that foreign land, away from all, Jawahar Lal Nehru felt lost. He sobbed, “And now we were left with only an urn of ashes of a person who was full of love and life.”

□

Rani Jhansi

Three children – two boys and one girl – were busy in playing on the Bank of the Ganges. One was engrossed in making forts with sand; another was assisting him in this while the third girl was exercising her small sword against some imaginary enemy. After a while all of them stopped their play and sat down to gossip.

The second one asked the first – "Well, Naana! What will you like to be in future?"

At this Naana stood up majestically and spoke like a warrior – "Oh, I will be the commander of my army to defeat the British force and win back our kingdom." His words and demeanour impressed his companions.

"And, what about you Chhabeeli?" This was asked from the girl whose beauty and bravery vied with each other. Her name was Manu Bai but she was called Chhabeeli by all. She was quick to reply – " I will be the queen and wrest back my kingdom from the English." She thought her no less than Naana with whom she had learnt the art of sword-wielding, archery, hunting and horse-riding. She was the daughter of Moro Pant who was Peshwa Baji Rao's Samant.

At her reply, Naana burst into a laughter – "Oh...ho...ho ! Look at this chip of a girl ! She wishes to be the Queen and fight against the mighty English?"

His words annoyed her. Anger flushed her pretty face and words came out like fire balls – "You are not the only one to fight the English! I have been always far better than you in sword-fight. Remember, Guruji always praised me!" So saying she turned away to go home in anger.

Her words had a ring of truth and proved to be prophetic. Manu Bai, got married to the king of Jhansi and thus she became Rani laxmi Bai, the queen of the State. But she had to prove her worth yet.

Destiny provided that occasion but in a cruel way. The king died after some time. As there was no crown-prince, Rani took over the reins of kingdom in her hands. She was only 25 then but she had the ability to rule. She proved to be very capable in her rule. She dressed like a man, attended the court, toured her state and strengthened the army. She added a new wing to it consisting of women named Laxmi Bai Regiment. She was the first to inspire and train women into warfare. This proved a great asset when they had to fight a battle against the British army. The state was being ruled efficiently but the British rulers were not happy. They wanted to annex the state of Jhansi and they got an excuse for that. Raja had died issueless. Therefore, according to the policy initiated by the viceroy Lord Hardinge, the state was to be annexed and ruled by the British Raj. Though Raja had adopted a son Damodar before his death, the British refused to accept him as crown-prince.

When the British Raj sent an order to Rani Lami Bai to handover her kingdom, she thundered like a lioness: "No, I will never give-up my Jhansi – come what may." The people had great love and regard for their Rani. They stood like a rock behind her. Rani was not alone in challenging the English. There was an uprising of the state against the British.

The British Raj was taken aback. It could not believe how a petty queen of a state could challenge the mighty British Empire.

But Rani had an iron will and a warrior's courage. Her army was strong and she was the Supreme Commander. She was like a Goddess to her people. They called her Durga and were ready to fight for their freedom to the last.

Sir Hugh Rose led a huge army against Rani Jhansi. But he found the whole route deserted of people, crops and water. He was amazed at Rani's wisdom who deprived his soldiers of food and water on way. The British soldiers suffered heavy losses. As the war began, Rani took command of her army. In a soldier's uniform with Damodar tied to her back, she was present at every front on horse-back.

Fierce war raged till seven days and nights. Rani proved a formidable force. But her army was dwindling; the fort wall was giving way to the enemy's canon-shells. The English were getting reinforcement from outside while Rani could not get any help from outside. Even Naana's soldiers could not reach her. She was trapped inside the fort.

At last all forced Rani to take an important decision to get out of the fort and reach the Fort of Gwalior to continue the battle from outside. The British tried hard to capture her alive. But she was like a lightning beyond their reach. She escaped out of the Fort with a group of selected horsemen. Sir Hugh Rose followed her. She was to reach Gwalior Fort but as ill luck would have it, her horse got stuck beside a rivulet, it could not jump over soon and the enemy shot from behind. Rani was wounded fatally...she could not survive the fatal attack.

She was carried by Ramchander Rav and a Pathan soldier into Baba Gangadar's hut nearby. As she had willed – 'No *firangi* should touch my body," her soldiers were quick to set the body on fire because the enemy was following them. With Damodar crying 'Ma...Ma...', they bade a tearful farewell to the great Queen of India. Her last words were नैनं दहति पावकः (No fire can burn the soul). She was the first and the best freedom-fighter of India.

□

In Gauri Temple

On that day Gauri Temple was abuzz with great excitement. All women of Jhansi were going to the temple in their best dresses. Their hearts were full of joy because today their dear Rani Laxmi Bai was coming to offer prayers there. They were anxious to meet the Rani.

These women were excitedly talking about her beauty, education and great warrior like qualities.

"How is it possible that a beautiful queen can handle a sword and ride a horse...?"

"We have heard that she has learnt how to use the bow, the sword and fight a battle. How can a woman do all this?"

Her question was answered by Rani herself who had entered just then and heard their talks.

All turned towards her – there stood Rani Laxmibai, resplendent in her dazzling beauty and smile! As they bowed to touch her feet, she held them with her hands and spoke sweetly – "No, not at my feet, but in my heart. You are just like my sisters." She embraced them.

They were overwhelmed with this love. One of them asked, "Rani Sahiba, please tell us, do you really do horse-riding and sword fight?"

"Of course, I do all this. And you can also learn to do this."

"Can we?" All spoke in one voice.

"Yes, you can learn if you want to...You must have heard the stories of Goddess Durga, Rani Padmini. Did not they learn this art of warfare?" The women were quiet for a while. Rani spoke again, "You must be thinking that a woman's place is at her home and her duties are towards her family. No doubt, you have to take care of home and children. But you should be brave enough to protect yourself and your country also when needed. And for this you should learn the art of warfare. Do not you want to defend your land while there are *firangis* ruling our country?"

At this, there was a commotion in them. Some young ones spoke – "Yes Rani Sahiba, we want to learn this...please, teach us horse-riding, sword-fight, archery-everything."

Rani was overjoyed to hear this. She said with a smile – "Today I announce my first battalion of women which will be called Laxmi Bai Regiment. You will be trained like a soldier."

"I offer myself as the first trainee..."

"And I, the second one..."

"And I, the third one..."

And their names were Sunder, Munder and Jhalkari. Thus, Laxmi Bai Regiment was founded and it played an important role on all fronts when there was a battle with the British army. It was the first women Regiment in History.

□

Sunder

"Oh my God! Even women are at the front...some carrying loading ammunition...some distributing food and water...some repairing broken walls of the Fort and some engaged in throwing cannon-shells !" The General of British force exclaimed while gazing at the Fort through his binoculors. He was full of wonder and praise for the Rani who had raised a strong women-force.

His roaming eyes fell on a tower named *Ochchi Phatak*. It was manned by Sunder and Dulhoju. They were throwing cannon-shells from that tower. The General gave a crooked smile. He instructed his men to raise a Red Flag before that Gate. On seeing that Flag, Dulhaju slowed down his cannon.

Sunder was manoeuvring another cannon from an adjoining tower. As Dulhaju's cannon slowed down, she looked at him with surprise: "Why has he slowed down while the enemy is facing us?" she thought with horror. But she was intelligent enough to notice the red flag before Dulhaju's tower. What does it mean? And in a moment its meaning flashed before her mind. It showed a sinister conspiracy in which Dulhaju was engaged with the enemy. As its meaning dawned at her, she was overpowered with anger and shame.

Because Dulhaju was not only betraying his motherland but also his wife. He was Sunder's husband.

Sunder's heart was in turmoil. Suddenly some previous incidents flashed before her mind—Dulhaju's absence from duty for no reason, his secret visits at night and meeting with a suspicious person PeerAli and now slowing down of the cannon – everything pointed to his treachery.

"Oh,God! Treachery towards Jhansi, towards Rani Sahiba...!" Sunder could think no longer. Immediately she drew out her sword and rushed towards Dulhaju. Her mind was racing...even a moment's delay could be disastrous - She saw from a distance that an enemy contingent had reached Orchcha Gate and Dulhaju was trying hard to break open the lock of the Gate. Seeing this Sunder flew like a tempest and the next moment she was at his head ready to strike.

Dulhaju's eyes met hers as if asking – "Why a sword over your husband's head?" Her eyes were ablaze with anger and guilt. She struck him with full force saying – "Shame on you for this betrayal...!" Dulhaju struck her back with the iron-rod, both fell dead and the Gate broke open to let in the enemy soldiers.

□

Munder

"Munder ! How can I bear to see my beloved Jhansi burning? Palace, temples, fort – all shattered by the British cannon – shells. These can be constructed again – but this burning library? Ah! Those books of great knowledge, the invaluable manuscripts...all burning to ashes! The treasury of books is gone forever." – so saying Rani of Jhansi wept bitterly. That valiant queen, who never lost heart even at the face of death, was unable to bear the loss of valuable library.

Munder, her soldier-companion who was always with her, consoled her – "Rani sahiba, our motherland asks for our supreme sacrifice...let's be ready to sacrifice all."

Munder was deputed with Raghu Nath on a tower which threw cannon-shells over the enemy forces. This reminded Rani of her other friend Sunder who gave away her life saving Orchcha Gate.

And now Rani, too, had to get out of the Fort so that she could get new arms and soldiers at Gwalior Fort to defeat the enemy. In this last journey Munder was also with her. A group of selected soldiers accompanied Rani. Their horses ran non-stop from Jhansi to Kalpi.... There was no time to stop as the enemy was following. As they reached near Gwalior, Rani's horse got stuck near a rivulet. It was not her old horse but a new one. She tried hard to push the horse but it took time and in that moment enemy bullet hit her from behind. Munder took that bullet over her and saved Rani. She fell from the horse with these words – "Bai Sahib...Pranaam..." Her husband Ragh Nath Singh sprang over the soldier like lightning and avenged his wife's death. Then, he tied her body with his Pagri (head-cloth) and putting it on horseback galloped on. There was no time to stop or shed a tear. In the next moment another bullet hit Rani on the head. She, too, fell down. Rani Laxmi Bai and her companion Munder's bodies were set on fire together.

□

Jhalkari

Setting Sun was casting its last rays over the fort of Jhansi. There was blood-shed everywhere and the dead outnumbered the living in this fierce battle between Jhansi and the British soldiers. Rani Laxmi Bai was standing at the fort; her heart was heavy as she looked around. Her beloved Jhansi was in the vicious grip of the enemy. Though she had put up a brave fight, still she knew her soldiers were decreasing, the Fort-walls were crumbling and the rations were finishing in the city.

"If only I could get help from outside? If Naana Sahib's soldiers could come to our rescue?" But that could not happen. Because the English army had encircled the Fort and did not let any help enter Jhansi. The British plan was to capture Rani alive so they were tightening their grip on the Fort.

"Rani Sahiba, we have to decide the only way to continue this battle and that is your escape from the Fort." An emergency meeting of selected people was called by Rani and this was the unanimous decision.

Rani knew this was the only way if she was to continue her battle.

"But...how can I leave without being captured?" This was the most difficult question which had no answer. All of a sudden, there stood a woman – "I have a plan Rani Sahiba."

All eyes were on that woman who was an officer of Laxmi Bai Regiment. Her expertise in warfare had endeared her to Rani. Rani smiled and asked, "Well Jhalkari, what do you plan to deceive the clever *firangis*?"

Jhalkari replied confidently: "Rani Sahiba, my plan is such as none except Your Highness can understand. Just look into my eyes and my face. You know I have a striking resemblance to you. Just honour my head with your headgear (Pagri of Queen) and I will be the queen of Jhansi for those *firangis.* And in those moments of confusion you can make good your escape from Jhansi."

As the plan was understood by all, everyone heaved a sigh of relief. Jhalkari had the same features, height and gait like the Rani. And she had her confidence and courage too.

"But, you know the result, Jhalkari? If and when found, you would be shot dead." Rani's voice trembled a little.

But Jhalkari smiled bravely – "Rani Sahiba, it was you who inspired us to be in Laxmibai Regiment. So how can I be afraid of death now?"

Now Rani had no answer. She embraced Jhalkari and placed her crowned Pagri over her head – "Go, Jhalkari, Jhansi will always remember your supreme sacrifice."

The plan was executed in no time. Jhalkari dressed up like Rani, mounted the best horse and plunged into the battlefield.

Recognising Rani's crown and face, the British soldiers encircled her. There ensued a big fight...all eyes were riveted to her.Taking her for Rani they used all force to catch her alive. In the meantime Rani Laxmibai made her escape with a group of officers.

There was great hue and cry when the British soldiers were able to capture Jhalkari in the name of Rani. There was great rejoicing. She was brought to the camp of the General. It was the proudest catch and Sir Hugh Rose's joy knew no bounds.

When Jhalkari's horse entered the General's camp, he got up to receive her while she kept sitting on horse – her head held high like the Rani that she was.

The General respectfully seated her beside him and spoke – "well, Your Highness..."

"No, no...This is not Rani Jhansi..." Like bomb-shell these words fell in his ears. There stood a traitor who had recognised Jhalkari. He came forward – "This is not Rani sir, she is Jhalkari...a soldier of Rani."

Jhalkari rose quickly to cut his head with her sword, but was caught by the General who was beside her. Seething with anger he shouted – "You...you cheated us...You will be shot dead..."

Jhalkari gave a hearty laugh – "And who is afraid of dying? I am the brave soldier of Rani Sahiba who has taken a vow to save our land from you 'firangis'."

General's companion Stuart asked her – "And why did you do this?"

"For our Rani Sahiba" – was the proud answer.

"She seems to be mad." Stuart said, "No, Stuart," interrupted Hugh Rose. "she is not mad...and if even one percent of Indian women become mad like her, we will have to run away from this land."

Then he ordered a special contingent of soldiers to follow Rani Jhansi. Jhalkari, too, embraced death with a smile.

□

Pan De Jethi

A strange drama was being enacted at the courtyard of a house in Deev Nagar of Kathiabar. People watched it with surprise. Beside a father's dead body, a Marriage-Mandap was prepared and the dead man's eleven year old boy was being married to a girl by Jethi Bai – wife of a reputed industrialist.

After the ceremony, the dead body was taken for cremation. Immediately after this, a Portuguese officer approached the inmates of the house to hand over the orphan-boy. But Jethi Bai came forward – "No, you have no right to take away the boy as he is married." After checking the proof of marriage, the officer returned blank. Now people were overjoyed to understand the whole thing.

It was an official practice in Deev Nagar that after the death of a parent, the orphan was taken into Government custody and converted to Christianity. Thus all the orphans were being turned Christians. The family of the dead suffered double loss. They suffered the loss of father as well as his son or daughter. Jethi Bai was an educated woman who understood the sinister plan of the ruler and decided to challenge it with intelligence. She started marrying the boy or girl before the cremation of his mother or father. In this way she could stop conversion of the helpless children. The oppressed people saw a ray of hope in darkness and Jethi Bai became an apostle of Hindu religion.

But the Portuguese rulers were unhappy over this. This woman had defeated them with her superior intelligence. Jethi Bai, too, was worried. She feared for the future when she would be no more to save these orphans. She knew at heart that a permanent solution lay in stopping this inhuman practice by the Governor. How to do it?

She thought of an excellent plan. One morning she boarded a boat and left for Goa. The journey took fourteen days. There was the danger of sea-storms and sea-robbers. But she had the courage of a lion and wisdom of *Saraswati* with her.

After reaching Goa, she appeared before the Governor's Residence in a strange attire. People gathered to see that woman who held a burning torch in one hand and a beautiful sandalwood box in the other hand. She carried a burning-stove over her head. Her cries of "Justice...Please, give me justice..." made the Governor come out. He was surprised to see a decent Indian woman in that strange attire.

He took her inside and asked – "What brings you here, lady? And what is the meaning of all this?"

Now Jethi Bai explained – "Sir, there is darkness of lawlessness in your regime – so I carry the torch in one hand; people are burning in the fire of cruel laws so I carry fire-stove over my head and in this box I bring an application from the oppressed people demanding justice from Your Highness." After this she opened the box and presented the 'Application' to the Governor. It was a piece of exquisite art – wrapped in the finest piece of Muslin-cloth which was beautifully embroidered and written in Portuguese language over an embroidered Lotus-flower.

The Governor was impressed by the personality of the woman who had travelled so far to fight against injustice for her people. Words of the application justified her cause. He sent it to the Queen with his recommendation. When it reached the queen, its exterior beauty caught her eyes while its interior beauty of subject-matter moved her heart. The words at the end of the long application brought tears to her eyes. It read - "Your Highness, you have the heart of a mother, just think over the plight of a family which loses its member to death and also a son or daughter to this inhuman law." The Queen was overwhelmed with love and regard for this lady who was fighting alone for this lofty cause. She immediately ordered - "This practice of converting the orphans be stopped immediately. Jethi Bai is awarded the title of 'My daughter'. The Royal Band would be played before her house and every officer will salute the lady while passing her residence."That historic application was titled "*Pan De Jethi*" by the Queen.

□

The Real Surrender

On Mandarachal mountain a sanyasi came out of the cave and sat on a stone to meditate for the evening prayers. Just then a young ascetic came there.

"Welcome, Sanyasi! Please accept regards from Shikhidhwaj," he said to the visitor.

The visitor replied, "Sanyasi Shikhidhwaj! Your name proves you to be a Kshatriya, not a Brahmin."

"Yes, Sir. You are right. I am a Kshatriya and I was the king of Ujjain 18 years ago."

This surprised the young sanyasi. He asked, "Then why did you renounce all and come to the forest?"

"I thought all worldly relations to be mortal. So I left them and came here to find that which is immortal."

"Well, Sanyasi, did you find that immortal one after doing penance for eighteen years?" He asked with a smile.

"No, Sir" Sanyasi replied with downcast eyes.

"And you will not be able to find that even in future," said the ascetic. Shocked by this prophecy, Sanyasi asked in a trembling voice," Why, Sir, what is lacking in my penance? I have surrendered my kingdom, pretty wife, my loving family and everything."

"No, Shikhidhwaj," he interrupted and said, – You are mistaken, you have not surrendered everything yet."

Shikhidhwaj failed to understand his words. He looked askance at him.

The young ascetic said again, "The royal family and the kingdom which you left, was not yours. It belonged to God. Everything you left, was already God's. So what did you surrender? You had nothing of your own then. But in this forest too, you have got many things to surrender." He pointed to his begging bowl, cloth-seat etc.

Shikhidhwaj hurriedly gathered these and went out saying, "You are right. I will surrender all and this cave too. I won't have any hut to live."

"Still there are some more things..."and his eyes pointed towards Shikhidhwaj's clothes, the rosary etc.

"Oh! I will leave all these too."

"There is something more to surrender. And that is the spiritual reward which you aim to receive for that penance?"

Hearing this Shikhidhwaj filled his palm with water and vowed to God, "I hereby surrender the reward of my penance" and poured that water on the ground.

"Shikhidhwaj! Your surrender is not complete until you surrender your body. It is not yours, is it?" the ascetic questioned with a mock smile.

Now Shikhidhwaj started to go out.

"Where are you going now?"

"Why, as you said, I am now going to surrender my body too." Hearing his words, the young sanyasi laughed heartily. Then he spoke – "Shikhidhwaj, you are still groping in the dark. The body, too, does not belong to you. It belongs to five elements i.e. water, earth, fire, air and the sky. The surrender of body is not your surrender. Your surrender means the surrender of the 'I' that resides hidden in your body. Until you surrender this 'ego' that 'I surrender', your surrender is incomplete and all your efforts of prayer, meditation or penance are meaningless."

With these words the young sanyasi left him. Shikhidhwaj stood stunned at this revelation of bare truth. A veil of darkness was lifted from his eyes and now this truth looked him in the eyes that all these years have been wasted in futile search. He understood that he had been in the wrong path from the beginning. It was wrong to renounce his duties as a king, husband and a son.

Now he ran out to find that wonderful Sanyasi who had shown him the right path. He found him sitting at a little distance. But when he faced him, he was wonder-struck. The ascetic had changed his dress and without the turban, Shikhidwaj recognised the pretty face of his wife! “Chuddala? Is it you? Is it a dream or a miracle?” Joy and surprise filled his words.

Chuddala replied calmly: “Swami, it is neither a dream nor a miracle. It is an example of my penance, my efforts to make you see the truth. You renounced all and went away avoiding your duties. But I could not do so. So I ruled over the kingdom and waited for your return. But you kept away for full eighteen years. So I had to play this drama and show you the right path of life.”

Shikhidhwaj was so overwhelmed with love and respect for her able wife that he could not speak. Then she spoke lovingly – “Swami, don’t avoid responsibilities. Work is real worship. By doing your work, you can realise the eternal truth of life. God has given you birth in a Kshatriya clan so that you may perform your duty to protect and provide for your people. Don’t shirk your duties. Remember the story of King Janak. If he could realise the eternal truth by doing his duties as a King, why can’t you?”

Now Shikhidhwaj had no answer. He bowed to her superior knowledge and holding her hands with love and gratitude returned to his kingdom.

□

The First Mathematician

A house in South India was being decorated with flowers and lights to prepare for the marriage of Leelavati who was the daughter of the renowned mathematician and astrologer Bhaskracharya. The girl had no mother so father had to perform double duties. He was very happy. Leelavati's marriage had been long due. But he could not find her a match. Though she was beautiful and very intelligent, yet her stars did not favour her match with anyone. When she was born, his father had written her horoscope . Then he came to know of this fact. She was born under such stars that she was destined to be a widow immediately after marriage. Father, being, an astrologer knew this eternal truth. So Leelavati could not be married so far.

Whenever he looked at her pretty face, he felt a blow on his heart. The young girl was withering away like a flower. He studied vast and worked hard to undo this cruel destiny. At last he succeeded in finding an auspicious hour when the marriage would be safe. He was quick to fix a match and prepare for the marriage.

Leelavati was sitting in the room wearing her bridal dress and ornaments. Her pretty face wore a look of anxiety. Her eyes were fixed on a Pitcher of water that was kept before her. There was another bowl which had a small hole through which the water was to pass into the pitcher.

When the pitcher would be filled, it will be the auspicious hour for Leelavati's marriage. Her father had devised this plan after consulting many books of Astrology. He had perfected it with his mathematical calculations.

Leelavati, too, had a great talent in mathematics. She knew this plan and so her eyes were at the water-pitcher. Her whole future depended on it. As she sat lost in thought, one pearl broke away from her earring and fell into the bowl and closed its hole. As destiny willed, the auspicious hour slipped away. Neither father nor daughter could come to know of this. So the marriage was solemnised with all rites. But no sooner did the bride enter her husband's home, destiny struck her. Leelavati came back to her father as a widow.

Father was stunned at her daughter's misfortune. He had tried hard to fight with her destiny but could not win. But he did not lose heart. He knew his daugher's sharp intellect and aptitude for Maths. He called her to sit beside him and held her hands – "Dear daughter, though a great misfortune had befallen us, yet we are not going to be finished. Being human beings, we are to live a life of fulfilment. Do not lose heart. You have a brilliant brain. Use your intellect in Mathematics for which you have an aptitude. You have the rarest capacity to study hard. I will also help you. Devote yourself body and soul into the study of Maths. The world might be lucky to have the first woman mathematician."

Inspired by her father, Leelavati put herself whole and soul into Maths. From morning till night both worked hard to discover and solve Mathematical problems. It was through sheer hard work that Sidhant Shiromani Epic of Maths was completed in which Leelavati's special contribution was in *Pariganit* that was named Leelavati by her proud father. On that day in tenth century the first woman mathematician was born.

□

Motto of a Warrior

Sound of war-trumpets filled the air of Sauveer State. King of Sindh had attacked the State. People and army got ready to give a befitting reply to the enemy. At the palace Queen-Mother Vidula waited anxiously for her son, the crown-prince Sanjay. She had the worship-plate in her hand to bless him before leaving.

When he came, she was shocked to see his pale face and slow pace. "What's the matter Sanjay? Are you afraid of the war?" she asked anxiously.

"No, mother. But I think that..." Mother cut him short, "No time to think now – it is time to *do or die*. The army is waiting for the commander to lead them to victory. Sanjay! gird up your loins and fight the enemy like a true soldier. Go soon." With these words she put *tilak* on his forehead and sent him away.

As the soldiers marched out of the capital, Vidula stood watching them from the palace-window. After her husband's death, she had put the responsibility of the state on Sanjay's shoulders who was strong in body but weak in heart. So Queen-Mother controlled and supervised everything. She was a lady of iron will.

After a few days as she stood waiting for good news from the battlefield, she heard someone whisper – "The prince has come back from the battleground." Her heart missed a beat. Before she could enquire further, Sanjay stood before her. His pale face and lowered eyes told the whole story. As he bent to touch her feet, she shrank back and thundered like a wounded lioness – "No, don't touch my feet. How dare you face me after showing your back to the enemy? Did I send you to the battleground for this cowardly escape?"

Sanjay faltered with these words – "But mother, the battle turned very fierce and I had to run away to save my life being your only son..."

"My only son?" Mother spoke in anguish. "No, Sanjay, you are not my only son, I am mother of all the sons who are risking their lives in the battlefield. And being the king, it is your duty to stand with them. How could you forget your responsibility towards your people?" Sanjay implored again – "But mother, I could be killed..."

Mother was quick to add – "To kill or be killed is the motto of a 'Rajput warrior' – Did you forget it? You have brought dishonour to the name of your brave father and forefathers. I feel ashamed to have given birth to a coward son who deserts his motherland when she is invaded. Sanjay, an honourable death in the battle-ground is far glorious than a life of slavery." And she turned away her face in utter disgust.

Mother's harsh words shook him to the bone. He felt as if a veil had been lifted from his eyes. And stark truth looked him in the eye. Now he saw clearly his fear of death was born out of cowardice and lack of responsibility. Guilt and shame overpowered him. He uttered these words – "Mother, I am going back and will show you my face only after victory."

As he galloped away, mother turned to look at his receding figure. With tears in her eyes and blessings on her lips, she prayed for his safety. Sanjay proved true to his words. He won victory but only after sacrificing his life for the motherland.

□

The Revenge

As King Dahar of Sindh fell dead in the battle against the Turk army, his army lost its ground. Leaderless soldiers were killed in no time. Victorious Turk commander Kasim entered the palace. Like a hawk, Kasim's eyes were searching for the beautiful queen. Soon he found her standing shocked in a corner of a room. Her two young daughters were with her. The news of her husband's death was so sudden that she could find no time to escape.

As Kasim advanced – his lustful eyes fixed at that pretty face, the queen acted faster. Like a lightning she thrust her dagger into her breast and fell down dead.

"Oh Khuda !" exclaimed Kasim – even his cruel heart trembled at the sight. But now he advanced towards the young daughters Sooraj and Parmal. They, too, drew out their daggers to kill themselves but now Kasim was alert – he rushed and overpowered them. The girls struggled hard but were helpless in his iron-grip.

Kasim laughed like a devil – "Ha ! Ha ! what a beautiful catch ! I will take you to Turkistan and offer to the Khalifa. He will reward me profusely."

He imprisoned them and sent away to Turkistan along with looted wealth in great security.

When Sooraj and Parmal were presented before Khalifa, their angelic beauty dazed his eyes. He could not believe such ethereal beauty existed on earth. "*Subhan Allah...!*" he exclaimed. As he stepped towards them, they shrank back - "Stop, Sir."

"Why? Why...stop now?" He smiled wickedly.

"Because...Sir, we are no longer worthy for your holy touch...we have been already molested by your commander Kasim..."saying this they hung their heads in shame.

"What? Kasim molested you?" Khalifa shouted in fury, "Are you telling the truth?" As he roared like a wounded lion, the girls looked up and replied in a strong voice – "Yes, Sir," and lowered their eyes as if ashamed to face him.

Now Khalifa could not wait a moment. He gave orders that Kasim be brought before him sewn alive in a leather-sack. This was the severest punishment. The order was immediately complied with. Kasim protested and entreated hard to be given a hearing before the Khalifa but he was denied this. As he was brought before the Khalifa – sewn in a leather-sack – he was dead due to suffocation. The Khalifa called Sooraj and Parmal and exclaimed proudly – "Girls ! Look at this damned son of a bitch! I have taken revenge for cheating me." And he laughed loud.

But the girls laughed louder and spoke – "No, sir not you but we have taken the revenge. Kasim had not molested us. This was our plan to punish him for killing our parents and for saving our honour from your unholy touch. Our revenge is complete now." And before the cheated Khalifa could punish them, they were quick to thrust their daggers into each other's hearts.

□

The Jewel

Maharani Durgavati ruled over the state of Garh Mandal. Though small, the state stood high in stature. The treasury was full of wealth, the people were prosperous. And it had a well-trained strong army to safeguard it from the invaders. The jewel of the crown was the Maharani herself. She ruled with an iron hand and a heart of gold. Though widow, she never let her grief come in the way of her duty. Her bravery surpassed her beauty. The state basked in her glorious reign.

But this independent, prosperous state was an eye-sore to the Mughal Emperor Akbar. He wanted to grab this state by hook or by crook. So he sent his messenger with this letter – "Shenshah Akbar is pleased to extend his hand of friendship to the Queen of Garh Mandal. He praises the Queen for ruling over the state efficiently though a helpless widow. The emperor wants the Queen to present herself at the Durbar with gift of jewels as a token of friendship."

As the letter was heard in the Durbar, all felt the sting of royal insult. The Queen kept her cool and asked in an unwavering voice – "Do you want to accept this offer of friendship from Akbar?"

All thundered in one voice – "No, never. We give a damn for such a humiliating offer!"

And the messenger was sent back with this reply – " Convey our words to your Emperor that he should not boast of being the Shenshah of Hindustan. There are many independent states like Garh Mandal who have the guts to defeat the Mughals. Garh Mandal is a land of the lions who are least afraid of the jackals. The Emperor should remember that the jewels are well-protected by the warriors of Garh Mandal."

After sending this reply Garh Mandal started preparation for the battle. Not only the soldiers but the people, too, got ready to give a befitting reply to Akbar. As they had challenged the proud Mughal, they understood the gravity of it.

As expected, Akbar sent a large army under the command of Asaf Khan. The invaders hit the walls of the Fort but could not advance an inch farther. The valiant soldiers led by Queen herself, struck back so hard that the invaders had to eat an humble pie and retreat.

But they attacked again. Now the battle was more fierce but the Rajputs fought with full force. Again, the attackers were defeated. Asaf Khan had never been defeated before. He could not fight another battle while Durgavati was commanding the army. He was terrorised by the Queen who fought with super-human courage holding swords in both hands. She was at every front to inspire her brave soldiers.

When Asaf Khan could not defeat the Rajputs in the front battle, he planned to strike from the backside. He tried hard to get hold of a black-sheep who may become a traitor. As ill luck would have it, one Rajput soldier fell into the trap. Money lured him and he struck his own soldiers from within. Now Durgavati's army was attacked from inside as well as outside. Between the two attacks, Durgavati proved her incomparable bravery. But it was an unequal fight as her soldiers were very few in number. First the crown-prince got killed and then the Queen was hit in the eye. But she kept on aiming at the enemy with even one eye. Akbar wanted to capture the Queen alive. But Durgavati acted fast. When they encircled her to capture, she thrust her dagger into her own breast and fell down dead. Akbar could only get some precious stones but not the real jewel of Garh Mandal.

□

The Queen-Mother

It was a glorious dawn. The rising sun was casting its golden rays over Shiv-Mandir. Devotees were on way to worship in the temple. A commander of the Rajput army was witnessing this from a distance. His camp was nearby. Suddenly he caught sight of a young girl who was holding the worship-plate and going towards the temple. Though a villager, she looked majestic. Her looks and gait seemed that of a queen. Her face had the glow of beauty and eyes showed strength of character. The commander was so impressed by her that he made enquiries about her. He was Malhar Rao Holkar.

After sometime that girl was married to Khande Rao and became the daughter-in-law of Senapati Malhar Rao Holkar of Indore State. She was like a jewel but her husband was not so capable. Father knew his son's weaknesses. So he called his daughter-in-law Ahalaya Bai to him and said, "Dear Ahalaya, you know your husband's inability to run the Kingdom. As I have to be away on military-trips, so I want you to learn the art of governing the state. I cannot bear the people suffer due to an inefficient King."

Ahalaya Bai bowed to his wishes and started her education as governor of the state. She was intelligent, diligent and kind hearted enough to become the perfect ruler. Now Malhar Rao felt assured about the State when he was away.

After nine years of living a life of bliss, Ahalaya received the first jolt of misfortune, when her husband died. She had two children and an old father-in-law to look after. But she decided to end her life as *Sati*-burning alive with husband's dead body.

As she stood in her bridal-dress beside her husband's pyre, Malhaar Rao came forward: "No, Ahalaya! You cannot do this."

She replied calmly – "Father, this is my duty. Please allow me to perform it."

"Duty towards the dead and neglect of the living?"

"Do you mean to say about my duty towards my children? But you are there to look after them father."

"No, I am not thinking of these two children but about hundreds of other children who live in our state. As a queen, you are mother to all those people. They have a right to be looked after. And you have a duty towards them as queen-mother."

Ahalaya Bai pondered over the wisdom of these words. The call of duty made her get down from the pyre. She held the spectre of the Ruler with strong hands and ruled over the state for many years. She faced many misfortunes – death of her father-in-law and her own daughter – but she never lost her patience. She reigned over Indore like Queen-Mother. Her rule is famous for good governance and prosperity in the pages of History.

□

The Dare-Devil

"Commander, prepare a formidable force to fight a fierce battle against that devil of a woman. We have to capture her alive." As Sir Malkum gave orders to his commander, his face mirrored his anxiety.

The Devil woman who had become a nightmare for the British rulers was Bheema Bai Holkar – grand-daughter of the illustrious queen Ahalaya Bai Holkar. She was Bheema (The Dare-Devil) not only in name but in her indomitable boldness too. She was well-versed in all warfare but her speciality was the guerrilla-warfare. She excelled in it to such an extent that even the wily British had to eat an humble pie at her hands. She struck at them at her own time and place and could not be caught so far.

Bheema Bai had not been such a dare-devil before. She had been a simple married girl a few years ago. But misfortunes struck her one after another. First her husband died suddenly. She started living a secluded life of a widow. Then her father died. She was trying to recover from these deaths when another bad news hit her. She came to know that the British were planning to grab the state of Indore. This was beyond her tolerance. She forgot her own grief and the loss of freedom for her entire state became most unbearable. She lamented – ”That dear motherland of mine which had been made prosperous by the blood and sweat of my illustrious ancestors like Ahalaya Bai Holkar and my father must be saved from the clutches of the foreigners.” She vowed to save her State and putting away the veil of a widow, there emerged a new Bheema Bai who became a terror for the British. As she could not prepare a large army, she trained selected soldiers in Guerrilla-Warfare on the pattern of Chchattarpati Shivaji. These Guerrilla attacks were so sudden and forceful that the enemy suffered a great loss.

But now General Malkum was himself leading a large army to the forest where Bheema Bai had her centre. His horse was nearing that place while his soldiers were advancing from all sides. Now there was no way through which she could escape.

Bheema Bai saw the advancing soldiers and understood the gravity of the situation. She ordered her soldiers to leave and save themselves. “But how can we leave you alone?” They sensed the danger to her life.

“Don’t worry for me. The British soldiers can never touch me.”She stood alone on her horse. Sir Malkum’s joy knew no bounds when he saw Bheema Bai all alone on her horse. He was moving nearer...his soldiers were encircling her now. He smiled proudly when his horse faced her horse – But the next moment like a lightning Bheema kicked her horse so hard that it jumped higher over Malkum’s head and galloped away like a tempest. It happened in a moment.

All were taken aback. None could believe his eyes. It was the rarest feat ever seen in horse-riding. Bheema Bai disappeared in the forest after her last dare-devil act of courage.

□

Hammir's Mother

"This way, Maharaj!" the horseman's words and eyes led the whole group through that field. They were accompanying the young King on a hunting-excursion. As the horses trampled through the field, someone shouted loudly – "Maharaj, please, stop the horses. My fields are ripe...we will lose the fruit of our labour for full year."

And there stood a young village-girl. The soldiers were impatient and angry – "But, you see, our hunted animal is lying beyond your field." Before the King could say a word, she promptly replied, "Maharaj please, wait here...I will bring your prey."

Saying this she went running through the field and after a moment came back carrying the dead wild boar on her back.

All watched her with eyes full of surprise and praise. As she turned to leave, the king stopped her – "Stop, brave girl! I must reward you for this extraordinary courage."

She smiled. "No Maharaj, this is in our daily routine when we have to save our crops from these wild animals. You are our King and I am happy to be of some service to you." She bowed to him and went her way.

On that very day the King was having his meal under a tree, when a stone came flying and fell near him. All stood up and looked for the offender. Next moment, same young girl came running and said with folded hands, "Maharaj, this offence has been committed by me. Without knowing your presence here, I aimed at the birds who were out to destroy my field...I beg your pardon, sir."

Her humble words brought smile to his angry face. He said- "Devi, we are again surprised and admire your courage and strength in defending your fields. We feel proud of your perfection in taking aim."

The girl again bowed her head in humility and went away. All talked about the farmer-girl whose bravery and perfect aiming were exemplary. Even the Senapati said, "I am not sure if any one of my soldiers can aim so perfectly?"

At this two soldiers stood up in protest – "Sir, this is not right – allow us to prove our worth."

One of their companion said in jest – "Are you ready to prove yourself today?"

"Yes, we are." At this the King and others burst into a merry laughter.

In the evening when they were returning, they saw the same girl going ahead. She was carrying a pitcher of milk over her head and holding the chains of two healthy buffaloes with both hands. She was walking in between the two animals.

These two soldiers looked at each other and requested the king to permit them for proving their superior ability.

The king permitted by saying – "Take care, the girl should not be harmed at all."

They rushed towards the girl. They aimed at passing through those animals so that the girl may lose her hold over them. As they neared her, she proved quicker and sensed their aim. She gathered her chains in both hands and struck with full force at their horses' front legs. The horses tumbled down with their riders while the girl stood majestically. This spectacle brought more praise from the king and all soldiers. Those two soldiers got up from the ground saying – "Maharaj, we bow to the superior strength of that girl."

The king's admiring look was fixed at the village-girl's back. He spoke to himself – "This girl would be the proud mother of an illustrious warrior."

He made enquiries and came to know that the girl was the daughter of a renowned Rajput warrior who was forced to lead his life as a farmer. The king could not forget that brave girl. He got married to her and his words proved true. She gave birth to the renowned hero Hammir Rao whose bravery was incomparable.

□

The Wedding Dress

"Maharani, the battle has become very dangerous. Our army is getting smaller and smaller–the enemy is advancing towards the Fort and Maharaj too..." But the brave Rani understood and completed it with courage, "and Maharaj sacrificed himself."

'Yes, Rani Sahiba." Maharani had no time even to shed tears. She ordered, "Bring me the best horse. Now I will complete the sacrifice of Maharaj."

With a vengeance Maharani of Gunnor Prabhavati plunged into the battle. In her leadership the soldiers fought like lions – inflicting heavy casualties to the enemy. But they had to leave the Fort and take Maharani to another safer Fort on the bank of Narmada river.

Maharani was continuing the battle from this Fort. But each passing day made them weaker. There was total disaster and arson in the Fort of Gunnor and it seemed sure that this Fort, too, would suffer the same fate.

Maharani was sitting lost in planning ways to win the battle, when a messenger from the enemy came with a letter. It read... "The Sultan proposes wedding with the Maharani."

This proposal hit like a dagger into her wounded heart. “Ah! If I could give a befitting reply to that devil” She uttered these words clutching her sword. But she knew that this was not the time for a show of might but of wisdom. So she controlled her emotions and thought of a plan. She sent this reply, “Yes, I am ready for the wedding. But you don’t have a wedding dress now. So I will send a suitable royal dress for your good self.”

The Mughal Sultan did not expect this. “A Rajput queen ready to wed a Nawab”– it had never happened. He was overjoyed to read this. After sometime a beautiful royal dress was sent by the Maharani.

It was night. All were asleep – some dead and some dead tired. In pitch darkness only the palace glimmered with lights. It was as if waiting for the royal bridegroom. When he entered the royal chamber, his eyes were dazed at the spectacle. The Maharani’s dazzling beauty outshone the decorated chamber. Feeling proud of his fortune, he exclaimed “*Oh Allah*! What a beauty you are!”

Maharani smiled – “Welcome Sir, please come to this bed – Will you have a drink?”

He could not believe his ears – “What? You would offer me a drink? How wonderful!”

“And...why not sir? After all you are a bridegroom and it is your wedding night,” so saying she filled a cup with wine and offered him.

While holding the cup, his hand shook a little and he uttered a low cry. Maharani asked “What is the matter Sir? Are you OK?” Her beautiful face showed worry.

By that time, his hand was shaking violently. The cup fell down spilling the wine. “Ah! Something is hurting me like thorns...ah! God! Are there thorns in the bed?” He cried in pain.

Now the Maharani had a hearty laugh. Her words rang in the room – “Yes Sir! There are thorns but not in the bed but in your wedding dress. You are wearing this special dress made of poisonous material. Now remember your God only because you are soon going to meet Him.”

"Oh, damn it! You sent me the poisonous wedding dress? I will kill you..." with these words, he rushed to her. But Maharani was too quick for him. She drew out her dagger and thundered, "Don't come near, you tyrant! How could you think that I would wed you who was destroyer of my kingdom and my dear husband? It was a revenge – a revenge wrapped in the wedding dress. My revenge is complete and now I leave for Heaven to be with my husband." And as the Nawab writhed in deathly pain due to strong poison, Maharani rushed out of the chamber and jumped into the Narmada River.

□

The Reward

"Do not go alone to the enemy camp," saying this Veermati stopped Krishan Rao.

"Why? Am I a coward?"

"No, you are not a coward. I have full faith in your courage. But it is not wise to go there because the enemy has received a humiliating defeat from us. So it can strike at you from behind." Veermati's heart was worried for her would-be husband.

"You are afraid for nothing. Rest assured, one Rajput is equal to ten persons. So no harm will come to me." Patting her hand lovingly Krishan Rao galloped away.

Veermati kept standing there. Her heart was full of love and pride for her brave beloved. She imagined that auspicious day when both will be united in marriage.

So she could not let him go unescorted to the enemy camp. She decided to follow him at a distance. On the way she passed through the battleground littered with dead bodies. Most of the soldiers belonged to Allaudin's army. The Rajputs had won a resounding victory under the warrior king Ramdev of Dev Giri Fort and Krishan Rao's name topped the list of brave soldiers.

As Krishan Rao's horse neared the enemy camp, she was surprised to see his horse go behind a bush. She could not understand that instead of going towards the camp, why has he entered the bush? She cautiously led her horse near the bush and tried to listen to slow whisper of Krishan Rao, "You may now attack our army because they are busy in merry-making,and if needed, I shall be at your side to help."

At this Mughal Senapati laughed heartily, "Oh well done! Sardar, you will be rewarded profusely by the Emperor. Just tell me..."

Veermati could hear no longer, her mind was in a whirl. She knew her king had sent Krishan Rao as his confidant to know certain secrets of the enemy. And here he was proving the greatest traitor deceiving his King, motherland and would be wife too. Her mind stopped working. Her horse advanced and her sword fell like lightning over Krishan Rao's head. Before the dazed enemy could do anything, Veermati struck the sword on her head too and fell down beside him. The traitor had been given his reward.

□

The Saviour

The wail of a child pierced the silence of the Arawali hills. There was such pain in it that it disturbed not only the forest but also a man sitting under a tree. He stood up and following the cries reached his hut. He saw his little child weeping bitterly in her mother's lap.

"What happened, dear? Why do you weep?" he asked taking the child in his embrace.

The child replied in sobs... "My roti...Billav...took away..."

He looked at his wife, "Why don't you give her another Roti?

She helplessly looked down on the ground. He understood the bitter truth. There was no other Roti.

He was the illustrious Maharana Pratap of Mewar who was at war with the Mughal Emperor Akbar. He had taken a vow to live in the jungle, sleep on the ground and eat only that green vegetable which could be found on earth. He had his wife and two small children. For many days his wife could get nothing to feed her children. So she cooked two *Rotis* of grass for them. When the child took her *Roti* to eat, a wild cat snatched it away. And now there was nothing to feed the hungry child.

This pitiable condition of the children tore his heart. His courage failed and grief and shame overwhelmed him. His mind went mad with this thought – "What an unfortunate father am I who cannot feed his children? What right do I have to make them suffer the pangs of hunger in this jungle? Why should we suffer such a wretched life? Should I let them die of hunger?"

This thought shook his very being. He got up immediately and took a paper and pen.

His wife watched him from a distance. As he finished writing, she approached him, "What have you written?"

He handed over the paper to her saying "Letter of Treaty to Akbar."

"What? – Treaty?—surrender? –" She saw him with a pained look and tore the paper into pieces.

"Why have you torn it? Should I let my children die of hunger? Should I not care for them as a father?" Rana's words were full of guilt.

Rani's face was contorted with anger, shame and pride. Her words came out like sparks of fire, "Yes, you are a father of these two children but you forget that you have taken a vow of being father to all the children of Mewar. You are a king who is responsible to feed and defend all people of your kingdom. How can you forget those innumerable soldiers who had shed their blood in the battles led by you against Akbar? What will become of all other children, men and women of Mewar state when you surrender to Akbar? Is it not a sin to surrender your Mewar for the sake of your own children? I won't let you commit this sin in this moment of weakness."

Rani's words flashed before him like sunlight in the dark. His eyes were opened to the truth behind her words. A new wave of courage travelled from toe to head. He felt as if he had woken up from a bad dream. Bowing before her, he spoke with pride "I am proud of you Rani. You have saved me from committing this sin in a fit of weakness. You have saved not only me but your Mewar state too."

□

The Ultimate Choice

In the prison cell of King Tailap Chalukya, King Munj was fretting and fuming like a caged lion – "I, the Prithvi Vallabh, sit here in chains who had defeated this Tailap not once, but thrice? Ah! What a wretched fate! But I won't stay here long...I would soon be free – there is no prison in the land that can keep me imprisoned for long. But the only thing which holds me in the prison is my darling Mrinal...Ah! why does not she come soon?" And the memory of his beloved brought a sweet smile on his face–his eyes closed with her loving images.

Marinal was his enemy Tailap's sister. Both had fallen in love forgetting that they belonged to sworn enemies. 'Love is blind' - proving this right, they kept meeting in the lonely prison-cell. No one could question or doubt her visit to the cell. It was only due to her presence that Munj felt the prison like a garden and had not tried to escape till now.

Suddenly there was a sound outside the wall. He stood up and tried to see. A man motioned Munj to come near...Munj recognised his man who had somehow sneaked to the place. He whispered - "Maharaj, we have constructed a tunnel underground.

We plan to take you out tonight after the first spell of night. Be prepared and vigilant." With these words he disappeared through that secret passage.

Munj stood overwhelmed with surprise and joy. So his men were intelligent and bold enough to free him from this cursed-cell. He already felt free like a bird.

But his happiness was clouded when he thought of Mrinal. He would have to leave without her. No, he cannot live without her. She was his very life...He would take her with him. "But will she come with me leaving his brother?" At this thought, his faith waivered... "Oh God ! what should I do?"

His question was answered by the beautiful Mrinal who had entered just then... "Dear Munj, I give you the answer. Now you should only love me ." And they were clasped in a passionate embrace. It was after a while that Mrinal asked smiling – "You seem to be worried a little. May I know the reason?" Munj was quick to reply – "In fact, Mrinal, it is only you who is the cause of my worry."

"Me ? don't you have faith in my love ?

Oh! No, darling, I have more faith in you than myself. I ask you Mrinal, will you love me till the end and come with me?"

"I do love you more than my life, but where do you propose to take me when you yourself are a prisoner?" She asked with mischief in her eyes. But Munj spoke seriously – "Mrinal, listen to me. I have a plan to escape from the prison tonight." And he divulged the whole plan to her. As she heard all, she fell silent. Her face lost its glorious smile and tears filled her beautiful eyes.

"Why these tears dear ? Don't you love me to come with me? Are you sad to leave your brother's home ?"

Mrinal could only whisper – "Yes" and then she stood up to go. Munj understood her situation and let her go to come back soon. He kissed her with the words – "Come sharp...after the first spell of night. But be very careful."

Mrinal rushed to her chamber and closing the door, burst into tears. Her heart was torn between love for Munj and love for her state. It was a choice between love and duty. She imagined her life with Munj full of love and prosperity but treachery with her motherland by letting the enemy free. Hours passed...she sat like a statue and then there was the sound of the gong announcing first spell of the night.

The sound struck her like lightning. She got up and stormed her way into his brother's room. Then she disclosed to him the whole plan of the enemy. When King Munj stood waiting anxiously for Mrinal, he was shocked to see his enemy Tailap instead of her. Next day King Munj was hanged to death. Mrinal had made the ultimate choice for her motherland.

□

At the Altar of Honour

"Taj Kunwari ! Go slow and watch your step !" One horseman addressed the other who was going fast.

"Why? What are you afraid of, brother?" She asked slowing down her horse.

"You know dear sister, this forest is very dense and Moghul soldiers keep hidden everywhere."

"But I have my sword ready for them. Don't you have faith in your sister's bravery?" She spoke excitedly.

"I do have enough faith in my brave sister. So I withdraw my words and beg pardon..."At this both burst into a laughter.

"Who goes there? Stop..." a shout echoed in the forest and there came out eight Pathan soldiers from behind a tree. They attacked both and were struck with equal strength. Five Pathans lost their lives. Now one fought with Taj Kunwari while two surrounded her brother. Suddenly Taj noticed one Pathan's sword ready to hit him from the back while he was fighting the other in the front. Taj Kunwari was quick to strike that Pathan in the back and thus save her brother's life.

Only one Pathan escaped while seven lay dead there. Both felt proud of their courage and swordsmanship. The brother embraced his sister and said affectionately, “My brave sister, today you saved not only my life but our honour too. I am proud of my sister.”

When they returned to their state, this news sent a wave of rejoicing in the people. They were the prince and princess of Kishora State. The king gave them a royal welcome. It was an occasion of great pride for him.

But the Emperor of Delhi fell into a rage when he heard the news from the escaped soldier. The free Kishora State had always been like a thorn in his eyes. Now he saw a golden opportunity to attack and annex the state. So a letter was sent – “Your daughter is guilty of killing our soldiers. Send her to us or face the consequences of a battle.”

As the letter was read to a packed Durbar, all rose in protest and thundered- “We won’t surrender our honour, but face the enemy with swords.” This resulted in a fierce battle between the two forces. But it was an unequal fight. The Emperor’s huge army crushed the small army of Kishora State. Though Rajputs fought with rare courage and bravery, even the king sacrificed his life. But they could not win the battle. Mughal army entered the Fort and started loot and arson. They advanced towards the Palace to capture the Prince and Princess. But both aimed at them with their arrows. Not a single soldier could advance further. The arrows hit them fast. Many soldiers lost their lives. But they kept advancing—slowly their circle grew closer. “Surrender now – or you would be captured – “shouted the enemy. They wanted to capture the Princess alive to offer to the Emperor. Prince Laxman Singh looked towards his sister Taj Kunwari – “Sister, now I am helpless to save you”. And he could not contain his tears.

Tajkunwari spoke bravely “A Rajput is never helpless Bhaiyya. Even now you can save your sister.”

"How?"

"By your sword - save my honour from the enemy."

"Yes, sister, I will save your honour." And taking a last look at her loving sister, he cut her head off and fell down killing many by the last stroke.

□

Token of Love

Amidst wedding music, the palanquin was brought in the courtyard. Ladies of the family welcomed the bride and took her inside. Mother of the bridegroom kissed her forehead and blessed the couple.

The newly-wedded couple sat for the performance of many rituals. It took quite long. It seemed like eternity when they got free from the priest. They were taken inside their room and left to each other alone.

Young hearts felt a sensation of love and excitement to be alone now. Both yearned to see each other – to touch – to feel the warmth of passion. As he unveiled her face, his eyes shone at the sight of her dazzling beauty. He held her in his arms and love engulfed both in a sea of bliss.

All of a sudden, *shehnai* stopped and loud sound of war-trumpets rent the air. They heard and understood its meaning. It was a call for the battle. Their arms left each other, lips parted in whisper," Oh—no—no!"

Rajput warrior stood shocked. He had to leave immediately for the battle. But he could not take his eyes off his newly wedded beautiful wife. His feet were glued to the floor – His bride stood beside him and putting the sword in his hand, said, "Why do you say 'No' Swami? Go and fight the enemy. I shall wait for you."

"Not today. I won't go – it is my wedding night."

Rajput wife held his sword in her hand and spoke with anger "Very well, you remain here to celebrate your wedding night but I leave for the battleground." As she stepped out, Rajput rushed to hold her back "Are you mad?"

"Yes, I am mad – but not for you. I am mad for my dear Mewar and I must go when it calls me."

Her words shook him strongly. He realised his weakness. Taking sword from her hand, he spoke bravely. "You showed me my real path. I am awakened to my duty. Let me go now. I will soon come victorious from the battlefield."

At this Rajput bride's face brightened up. She heaved a sigh of relief and prayed to Goddess Bhawani to defend her husband. He was the valiant Choodavat Rajput and she was his Haari Rani. It was the rarest occasion that he had to leave his bride on the very night of wedding.

She stood at the window looking at his husband on horseback. He, too, looked towards her. As their eyes met, he felt a strange sensation in his body. He stopped the horse and sent a messenger to his wife. The messenger said – "Raniji, Choodawatji has asked for a token of love to take along."

"Token of Love" these words were enough to speak about the love-lorn heart of her husband. She understood that his feet were tied to her. It was her attraction that lured him back. He was unable to leave her and go to the field. This infatuation was killing his brave spirit – "Who was keeping him back from duty? Who was making him a coward?"

She knew the answer. In an instant she took the boldest decision.

She spoke to the messenger. "Wait, I am giving you this token of love for him," saying this she drew out her dagger and cut off her head. The messenger's eyes were dazed to look at the horrible spectacle – Haadi Rani stood offering her severed head to him to take away for the Choodawat Rajput. Like a mad man he rushed back to Choodawat Sardar and offered him the blood dripping head of his wife. All eyes were shocked to see this strange scene. Choodawat's heart was filled with love for his brave wife but his guilt ashamed him. He wore her head in his neck and fell like lightning upon the enemy forces. No wife had ever offered such a token of love to her husband.

□

Another Rukmani

Rainbow colours adorned the portraits of princes and kings. These were being presented to the princess of Roopan Garh by a woman-seller. The princess and her friends were watching and giving their comments at each photograph.

"And whose portrait is this?" The princess picked one from the heap. She was gazing at it with eyes full of admiration.

All eyes turned to it and there was an uproar – "Oh, what a handsome Prince ! Look at his glorious face and the proud look! He reminds us of Maharana Pratap..."

The woman was quick to remark – "Yes, you are right. He belongs to Rana Pratap's Clan. He is Rana Raj Singh of Mewar!"

"Rana Raj Singh...descendant of illustrious Rana Pratap!" the princess kept repeating the name in her heart. The more she looked, the more she loved that handsome Rajput.

"Now have a look at this grand portrait of Alamgir Aurangzeb Badshah"– saying this the woman showed a beautifully framed photograph of Emperor Aurangzeb.

On seeing that photograph, all burst into laughter exclaiming – "Oh, what a piece of beauty is the Alamgir! Look at the ugly face!" as they spoke and passed the photograph from one hand to another, it fell down and broke.

The woman, being a Muslim, was shocked at the sight. She could not control her anger and said, "Such an insult of your King's photograph. If ever he comes to know of it, your state will pay heavily for it."

The woman's words hurt the proud princess, she exclaimed in anger – "No, he is not our King. He is an invader who has come to loot our country." With these words she paid the price for that photograph and said to her friends – "Now, come and hit this photograph with your foot. Let us see his power!"

With these words the princess hit the photograph with her foot and everyone did the same. The frame was shattered to pieces. The woman was too shocked to speak. She packed her things and left.

The princess had the portrait of Rana Raj Singh which had sowed the seed of love in her young heart. She was enamoured of his bravery as well as beauty. She had dedicated her maiden's dream to her dream-hero. But destiny willed otherwise. As Aurangzeb came to know of this incident, he was beside himself with rage. " How dare a petty state challenge the mighty Emperor? How could the chip of a girl insult his photograph? She has to be taught a good lesson for this." He fumed and ordered to bring the princess to his palace. A large army was sent towards Roopan Garh.

'Send the princess or fight the army'– was the only choice put before the king of Roopan Garh. The king got so afraid of the army that he chose to send his daughter to Aurangzeb. But the princess refused to accept this. Father entreated his daughter expressing his inability to fight the mighty army but his daughter was adamant. She said – "I will prefer death to dishonour at the hands of Aurangzeb." She offered to commit suicide by fire or poison. But the king forbade her to do this because he knew its result. It would enrage Aurangzeb to attack and destroy this small state.

"Now, you tell me what should I do?" The princess wept bitterly before her beloved's photograph. All of a sudden, she had an idea. She wrote a letter to Raj Singh and sent it immediately.

The letter reached his hands. It read – "Mewar King Rana ji, you are the worthy descendant of the great Rana Pratap who never bowed his proud head before the invaders. Will you let the tyrant Aurangzeb humiliate a Rajput girl who has dedicated herself to you? I offer myself wholly at your feet like Rukmani in the past. Come to me like Krishan and take me with you before that cursed king snatches me away. I will prefer death to dishonour."

The words were like sparks of fire. They had the desired effect. Raj Singh's heart swelled with love and pride for his wouldbe wife. He thought of a clever plan and informed the princess.

The princess sat in the decorated palanquin as a bride and left amidst the soldiers. She was gazing outside through her veil to see her saviour. Her whole life depended on this. This could be her last journey to life or death. Suddenly there was a thunderous sound. Raj Singh's hidden soldiers had attacked the enemy while they were passing through a narrow passage. The enemy was taken unawares. The attack was so sudden and ferocious that they could not face it longer. And Rana Raj Singh happily took away his bride as Krishan had taken Rukmani.

□

The Lioness

"Soldiers! This is our last night in the Fort. You know the Fort has been under siege since last week. We fought the enemy with all strength but now we are left with only a few soldiers and broken wall of the fort. So we have to take the final decision to open the gate and die fighting. This is the only way."

"No Sir, there is one more way, " a woman's voice interrupted Senapati.

"What?" he turned towards the woman with a new hope in his eyes. He recognised her. She was Harsharan Kaur, known for her rare courage and intelligence. She came forward– "Sir, if we are able to send a message to Senapati Hari Singh Nalwa at Peshawar, he will immediately come to our help and defeat the enemy from outside."

On hearing this, the light died in his eyes and he said in desperation, "The plan is good but who will carry the message? No one can get out of the fort without being killed by the Pathans."

"Sir, leave this task to me. I will carry the message." On hearing her bold words, all held their breath. Senapati spoke. "Sister, your courage is praiseworthy. But I cannot allow you to go into the jaws of death and dishonour at the hands of Pathans when your Singh brothers are alive?" Harsharan smiled bravely "I am proud of my loving brothers but I have a foolproof plan which will succeed without harming me." This surprised the Senapati. But when he heard the whole plan from Harsharan, he, too, became confident of its success. He permitted her to execute her plan.

She aqueezed her slender body to fit in the garb of a dog and walked on her hand and feet like a dog. This master plan was the first of its kind to be ever thought of and executed successfully by a woman. As night fell, the gate of the fort opened a little. As the Pathan soldier held his gun high to shoot, he saw a dirty dog walking out slowly. With a sneer, he kept the gun down.

The dog kept walking, first slow, then fast and faster. When out of reach of the enemy, it straightened itself and there stood Harsharan Kaur—under the garb of the dog. Now she started going fast because the journey was long and hard. But she reached Peshawar before daybreak. As the letter reached Hari Singh, he read it and roared like a wounded lion, "How dare the Pathans grab our fort? Jamrod Fort belongs to us and none can touch it as long as Nalwa is alive." Though sick, he got up and soon prepared to lead the army towards Jamrod. "But who brought the message while the Fort is in siege?"

"A woman, Sir." Hearing this, he rushed out and saw a young girl sitting tired beside the door with eyes closed.

"Blessed be the daughter of Punjab! That is why Punjab is called the land of lions." As he spoke, Harsharan opened her eyes and rose to bow at the feet of the Lion of Punjab, Hari Singh Nalwa. But he caught her hands and said with affection, "No sister, it is your blessed feet which deserve to be touched. I bow my head to the brave lioness of Punjab."

Now Hari Singh Nalwa lost no time. His horse flew towards the Fort with his soldiers. 'Nalwa has come' this war-cry was enough to scare the life out of the Pathans. Nalwa's soldiers struck like lightning and the Pathan soldiers were killed in no time. When at the Fort, Hari Singh Nalwa took along brave Harsharan Kaur with him and said, “Sister, Jamrod’s victory will always remind all of her illustrious daughter, the Lioness of Punjab.”

□

Words of Fire

A dazzling beauty looked out of the crystal mirror. Her angelic body was as if crafted with petals of pink roses. Her pristine beauty astounded the onlooker. As she stood majestically with a bewitching smile, a heavenly glow emanated from her body.When he looked at her he forgot everything – he forgot that he was Sultan Allauddin and had promised the Rana to have only a look at his queen. In fact, he could only remember that dazzling beauty whose name was Padmini and who belonged to Rana Rattan Singh of Chittor.

"No, she should belong to me – she will be only mine". with this resolve he travelled back from Rana's palace. But how to get her? He knew the Rajputs were proud and brave enough to cut off any hand that touched their women. He could never win her by the power of sword. "But there is another way"– he thought of a clever plan. Rana had accompanied him to bid him a friendly farewell. Allauddin snatched this opportunity and took Rana into captivity and drove away from Chittor.

A message was sent to Chittor "If you want Rana alive, send Padmini to Allauddin immediately." As the message was read out in the Durbar, it fell like a bomb- shell. The valiant Rajputs were up in arms, ready to fight Allauddin. With one voice they spoke – "Not our Rani, but death will meet you on the battle ground."As the messenger turned to leave, Rani Padmini's voice echoed in the hall – "Stop – tell Allauddin that I will come." All were shocked to hear Padmini's words. They could not believe their ears. After a moment Badal – Rani's brave brother, dared to ask, "But Maharaniji, what are you saying?"

Padmini cast her calm look at all and said, "I know you are surprised and pained at my decision, but you must remember that we may win the battle but will surely lose our king. We are faced with a dilemma to choose between Rani or the King of Chittor."

"But even Ranaji will never allow us to send you away."

"Yes, I am fully aware of this.Therefore we should face the enemy not with arms but with wisdom."

All bowed before Rani's wise suggestion. They thought of a clever plan. According to it Padmini would go to Allauddin's place accompanied by her seven hundred friends sitting in Palkis. Secondly, she would meet her husband alone before going to Allauddin's Harem.

Allauddin was overjoyed to receive the message. No condition could be great enough for the prized possession of Padmini. He immediately accepted the conditions.

Next day a strange sight was witnessed by the people. Rani Padmini's decorated Palanquins came out of the gate of the Fort followed by seven hundred Palanquins and advanced towards Allyudin's place. It was a sight that shocked everyone. After reaching the destination, Rani's Palanquin went to Rana Rattan Singh while the rest waited outside.

When Rani took long with her husband, Allauddin got impatient and sent a messenger to bring her. But before he could reach there, loud war-cries of "Maaro-Pakro-Kaato" (Kill...Catch...cut down) filled the air. The enemy was taken unawares. Seven hundred Rajputs who were sitting in the Palanquins with their arms accompanied by bearers made a battalion of 3500 warriors who struck at the enemy with full force. The enemy was routed in no time. Though the valiant Rajput warrior Badal had to sacrifice his life, yet her sister Padmini safely got Rana free from prison to Chittor Fort.

Allauddin was seething with anger and felt cheated. Padmini was snatched away from his clutches along with Rana. He commanded a large army and attacked Chittor with a vengeance. The Rajputs were prepared for this attack. They fought to the last. But as the enemy outnumbered them, it was decided by Rana that the Rajputs had no other alternative but to open the gate and fight the enemy in the last battle. The Rajput men left the fort to fight the last battle with the enemy and fourteen thousand Rajput women along with Rani Padmini prepared for *Jouhar* (self-immolation). Padmini – that dazzling beauty bedecked like a bride, first embraced fire followed by all brides. When Allauddin entered the Palace as a victor, he could see only the flames which had written the immortal story of Padmini in words of fire.

□

A Little Girl's Vow

The crown of the temple was struck hard by the invader's blow. It crumbled to pieces. Then the walls were pulled down and lastly the Holy Idols were broken into pieces. Only a few moments ago, there stood the temple in its majestic glory and now there was only dust of broken stones. The eerie silence was echoing with the invader's cruel laughter.

A girl witnessed this from a distance. She had a worship-plate in her hands to worship in the temple. She was coming from a far off village. This scene of destruction stopped her feet. She felt as if the invader's blow struck at her heart. The pain brought tears to her eyes. The dishonour of sacred idols hit her with a pang of sorrow and anger. She wanted to strike back at the invader. But how could she face that giant swordsman with her little hands?

Helplessly she wept piteously. Holding the broken idols of Goddess she vowed "Mother, I pledge to take revenge on the invaders."

Time passed. That girl grew and her will to take revenge, too, grew stronger. One day she told her father about the incident and exhorted him to punish the invader. Father expressed his helplessness to face the invader who was representative of the Moghul Emperor. The girl got married. She expressed the same desire to her husband. He, too, proved weak and helpless. But she did not lose heart.

Now she put all her hopes on the son she was going to have soon. And it was a day of fulfilment of her dream when a boy was born to her.

She was the proud mother Jija Bai who gave birth to Shivaji. From the very beginning she inculcated in him high ideals of patriotism, respect for religion, cow, women and places of worship. She told the child heroic tales from Ramayana, Mahabharata. She moulded him in the frame of a warrior who was born to fulfil the aim of saving his country from the invader. Jija Bai took him into the temple and he vowed before Goddess Bhawani to defend his country and religion. Shivaji rose to be the best warrior of his time. He invented a new type of warfare called 'the guerrilla warfare'. His successful guerrilla attacks struck at the very root of Moghul rule in Maharashtra State. He established Hindu Pad Paadshahi in the state driving out the Moghuls. That fulfilled Jija Bai's vow to Mother Bhawani. A little girl's determined efforts created that great hero of Indian history: Chhattarpati Shivaji.

□

Test of Love

There was great hustle and bustle in Chittor Fort that day. Groups of Rajputs were on way to the battleground to defend their motherland from the Moghul invaders. Every soldier got blessed from his mother, sister or wife at home. So he had *Tilak* on his forehead. Flower petals were showered on the way.

A group of women was standing at a door waiting for the warriors. One addressed the other – "Viddul, where is your beloved one? Why is he not coming?"

At this Vidull's pretty face got flushed. Before she could reply, another said in jest – "He must have forgotten to go to the battle - ground while thinking of his beloved Viddull."

Now Viddul's face was red with shame and anger. But before she could reply back, a new group of soldiers was seen advancing forward. As Viddul saw the Rajput leading the group, her face turned crimson with joy. He was her betrothed Samar Singh who was to wed her after his return. As the horse-men stood before them, they raised their worship-plates with lighted lamps, saffron and flowers – blessing the warriors to come back victorious. Viddul's eyes gave him a silent message – "First win victory and then win your bride."

After this, time hung heavy on all who were at the fort waiting anxiously for the battle to end victoriously. Viddul spent her days praying to God that victory may bless the Rajputs.

Days turned into nights and time wore on. One night Viddul was standing in her courtyard. Her eyes were gazing at the moon – thinking of her own moon who was far away amid danger of death. She was torn between thoughts of sorrow and joy. When she imagined her coming wedding, her heart danced with joy but imagining death and disaster at the battleground, she trembled with sorrow.

Suddenly she heard a sound from behind. She turned back and raised her dagger to a shadow but after coming near, she was too shocked to speak. It was Samar Singh.

"You...? Here...? Is the battle over?" she asked anxiously.

"No, Viddul, the battle is not over yet...but I just sneaked away to see you —".

"You sneaked away to see me—" as she repeated his words, her anger rose like fire and engulfed her whole being. Trembling with anger and shame she thundered, "How could you do this Samar Singh? How dare you turn your back to the battle ground to see my face? You are a coward and I feel ashamed of myself."

Samar Singh's face fell. He hung his head in shame and said, "I am sorry Viddul but I was helpless. Your love..."

Interrupting him, she thundered, "Not my love Samar but my hatred for you if you come back as a coward. A Rajput wife weds a warrior – not an escapist coward. Go away – Viddul is dead for you." So saying she ran away blinded by tears of shame and sorrow.

Samar Singh went back. The battle raged more fiercely. There was death and disaster everywhere. The Rajputs were winning at first. Suddenly battle turned worse for them. Rajputs were being slaughtered like hunted animals. There were cries of wailing mothers and wives as the news of defeat reached Chittor. Now there was no other way to save their honour from the invaders. So Rajput women decided to embrace fire in *Jauhar*.

A huge fire was lit in the fort and all women bedecked themselves as brides. Because it was not an occasion for sorrow but pride and bliss to follow the path of their men at war. Viddul, too, was dressed like a bride though not wedded yet.

"Stop, stop Viddul, I am here". someone came running while shouting. Viddul looked up. There he was Samar Singh – her would be husband. Her heart missed a beat. He was alive But how? And then, she saw the Moghul soldiers accompanying him like an escort. Now she understood everything. Samar Singh had turned a traitor and was a tool in the hands of the enemy. That was the reason of Rajput soldiers' victory changing into a defeat in the end.

Viddul's head hung in shame – her heart broke with guilt of being a traitor's betrothed. She leapt like a wounded tigress and thrust her dagger into Samar's chest with these words – "Traitor! This should be your reward." Saying this she jumped into the flames of *Jauhar*.

□

For the Motherland

"I can't bear it more, brother." As he set foot in the home, he was shocked to hear her sister's words.

He instantly went near her and asked anxiously, "What can't you bear, sister?"

Before words could come, tears ran from her swollen eyes. It was clear that she had been weeping since long. She was Khandowal's young widowed sister living with him. Without husband and parents, she had only her brother. But he looked after her with great affection. So he could not tolerate her grief. "Tell me dear sister, who has brought tears in your eyes? Disclose his name and your brother will wipe him out of this world." He knew his sister had great patience and never got disturbed by small reasons.

With downcast eyes she spoke in a trembling voice, "Bhaiya, Raja Sambhaji again came here yesterday evening." saying this she burst into heart-rending sobs.

Her words hit him like a dagger. Their hidden meaning filled him with shame and anger. Unable to face his sister, he turned away and hid his face with his hands.

Raja Sambhaji was ruling the state of Maharashtra as Chhattarpati Shivaji's son. But he was his son only by name. Otherwise his character was just the opposite. Unlike Shivaji, he ruled like an ordinary king full of all the vices. His loose character and cowardice disappointed all able chieftains of Shivaji and they had drifted away from him. Sometimes, he, too decided to oppose and leave Sambhaji. But if left alone, the Moghul enemy will attack the weak king and win over the State. Only this fear for the state kept him with Sambhaji. He could not bear the Hindu Raj that Shivaji founded with his bravery – to be annexed by the enemy. It was like a sacred temple built by the sweat and blood of many swordsmen led by Shivaji. How could he let it crumble down to pieces?

But now Sambaji's sinister advances towards his sister made him mad with anger. His hand tightened over his sword to cut off the head of the immoral King. But as he stepped out, a strong thought stopped him. "When the King is killed, there will be lawlessness and it would invite the enemy to attack." And this pulled him inside. He could not let go of his state to the enemy. Then what was the way?

"Sacrifice–sacrifice for the motherland was the only way." He steeled his heart and stood before his sister with a cup of poison. "Sister dear, pardon your helpless brother who offers you a cup of poison to end your life to save our motherland." Tears blinded his eyes. But she held the cup with a strong hand and said in a calm voice – "No, Bhaiya, do not feel sorry for me. I am your sister and feel proud to be of some use for our motherland.

□

Meena Bazar

"What a magnificent scarf! Just look at the exquisite embroidery! And these stone-studded bangles...see, this star-studded Dupatta...I want to have all these..." She was chattering merrily. But her companion was not listening.

"Oh, Kiran, where are you lost? You are neither seeing nor listening to anything in the Meena Bazar." At her words, Kiran woke up from her reverie. Indeed, she was lost in her own thoughts – her mind painfully thinking about the hideous darkness that lay behind this bright Meena Bazar.

It was the occasion of Nau Roj Fair. The market was overfilled with shops selling glittering things of cosmetics, jewellery, clothes etc. to the women folk. This was the notorious Meena Bazar opened by the royal order of Emperor Akbar. Here only women came and shopped freely.

"Only women!" Kiran muttered with disgust, "what a farce! That detestable cheat must be roaming about hidden in a woman's *Burqua"* and with this thought her blood boiled in anger.

"Rani Sahiba, let me show you some special bangles. Please, come with me" – a soft hand touched Kiran's shoulder with these words. She turned and faced her. It was the same woman who had been following her when she had entered Meena Bazar. Kiran understood everything. As her friend was busy somewhere, she immediately accompanied the woman. The woman led Kiranwati into another room through that shop. Kiran touched her hidden dagger before entering the room. Though glass-bangles shone from the almirahas, still the room did not look like a shop. It was like a well-decorated fort with only one door. The woman started showing off pretty bangles. As Kiran did not like them, the woman went to bring some better bangles.

Now Kiran was all alone in that room. With abated breath, she sat waiting for the next moment. She had entered the lion's den, but she, too, was not an ordinary woman. She was the daughter of Rana Shakti Singh – younger brother of Rana Partap Singh. She was married to the great warrior Prithvi Raj. Besides angelic beauty, she possessed the courage of a lioness. She had entered this Meena Bazar with her indomitable courage and an iron will.

"*Wallaha* ! What a great beauty...!" These words broke the silence and she saw Akbar entering the room from some hidden door. She got up like lightning and stepping towards Akbar, hit him hard at the chest. As he fell down she immediately nabbed him under her foot and put the dagger to his throat.

This happened so quickly that Akbar could not do anything. He struggled hard to get up but Kiran had put her whole weight – physical as well as mental – in her grip, she did not let him escape. Pushing the deadly dagger deep, she thundered, "You! the cursed king of Delhi! Now you will have to atone for all the sins you have committed in this Meena Bazar. You will pay with your life for dishonouring Rajput women. Like a jackal you hunted for them hidden in a woman's guise. Shame on you! Today I have come to punish you" and she pushed the dagger deeper.

The Emperor cried in pain – "Oh, forgive me...Mother. I entreat you like a child to pardon my sins. I vow with my life to close this notorious Meena bazaar forever. I will never ever cast a look at any woman." Tears of shame and sorrow ran over his deathly-pale face - with a fallen pride, he was begging for life.

Kiranwati put away her dagger and said, "Akbar, you called me Mother. This word means a lot for a Rajput woman. With a mother's heart, I pardon you and grant you life. But remember your vow till the end otherwise Kiranwati won't pardon you second time."

Leaving him on the floor, she went out like a whirlwind. Her beautiful face shone with a heavenly glow at the fulfilment of her mission. History testifies that Akbar closed the Meena Bazar forever.

□

The First Missionary

Patiliputra, the capital of Emperor Ashoka's Kingdom, was wearing a festive look. The occasion was the Coronation-Ceremony of the Crown prince Mahendra. Kings of other states were reaching the capital with royal gifts. The Darbar hall was looking bright and gorgeous. The Emperor sat proudly at the throne. He looked towards his son with fond eyes. All hearts where expectant with the coming happy moments.

When Acharya from Budha monastery entered the court, all stood up and bowed before him. The king spoke reverentially – "Acharyaji, how is your work going on? Do you need any help to preach the gospel of Budha?"

"Maharaja ! You have provided generously for the cause of Dharma. So we do not need any wealth for it but we do need one thing acutely..."

"And what is that? Please, mention it and I will provide it immediately. You know, sir, I, along with my whole kingdom is at the service of Budha Dharma. What do you need sir?" King's deep faith spoke in these words.

Acharyaji kept thinking. Then he looked first towards the

prince and then to the king and said, "Maharaj ! we need a young, educated missionary to devote himself in preaching Dharma far and wide, and for this there is none more capable than Yuvraj Mahendra."

"Yuvraj Mahendra?" – Ashoka repeated the words as his throat got choked and eyes became moist. As the meaning of these words sank into his mind, his whole world came crashing down. That beautiful dream of the coronation of the prince lay shattered. Even the imagination of Mahendra turning into a monk tore his loving heart. He could not speak.

Prince Mahendra understood his father's grief. He knew his dilemma who was torn between the love of son and commitment to Budha Dharma. So he came forward and bowed before his father, - "Respected Father, don't grieve for me. Your teachings have already made me a devotee of Budha. I am fortunate to be chosen for this missionary-work of Dharma. It is no less honourable than the Coronation."

His words felt like soothing balm on the grieving heart of the father. Now he took control of his emotions and gave Mahendra's hand into Acharya's hands saying – "Acharyaji, here is your worker. I dedicate him to the blessed cause of Dharma. Let him take these lofty ideals to far and wide."

Acharyaji was too pleased to speak. He blessed the Emperor with a grateful heart. The news spread like wildfire in the state. The crown-prince abdicating the throne to become a monk of Budha Dharma was unthinkable and unbelievable. People were reminded of another such sacrifice when Ram Chandra had abdicated the throne of Ayodhya to fulfil his father's vow. Mahendra's sacrifice surpassed even Ram Chandra. As soon as his sister Sanghmitra heard the news, she came running to the court.

"Dear Father, my brother is allowed to devote his life for the cause of Lord Budha, I ,too, want to devote my life for this."

Father's heart, again, felt the blow. Perplexed he asked – "You, too, daughter?." He could not believe that a young girl of great beauty was ready to renounce the world for the sake of Dharma. Her pretty face shone with the determination. Ashoka could not but allow her to follow her illustrious brother. Both were initiated into the organisation at the Monastry. They were deputed to travel to Sri Lanka and light the lamp of Budha's gospel there. Mehendra's missionary work had a great impact on the people. When the princess of Sri Lanka decided to embrace Budha Dharma, Sanghmitra felt the fulfilment of her missionary work. The princess was initiated into the Dharma along with five hundred women.

Sanghmitra was the first missionary who went out of her country to work for Dharma.

□

The Eternal Star

After sending her son Dhruv to the capital with sanyasins, Suniti stood at the door, lost in thought—"Would the king welcome his son after so many years? How happy and proud would the young prince feel to see his own palace and capital? How queen Suruchi..." and this word broke the chain of her pleasant thoughts.

Name of Suruchi brought back bitter memories of the past. She had not forgotten the cruelty of Suruchi, second wife of her husband. As she was praying to God to avoid ill luck, she heard the sound of running steps. As she looked up, she saw Dhruv running to her in an agitated state of mind. As soon as he came near, he collapsed into her arms weeping.

Mother's heart felt a hard blow. She embraced the sobbing son and asked – "What happened Dhruv? Did anyone hit or insult you?"

Dhruv was too shaken to speak. His companions related the whole incident that when Dhruv reached the King's Court, he affectionately took him in his lap. But after a while Queen Suruchi rushed into the court and pushed Dhruv down form his lap, saying "A beggar's son is not entitled to sit in the King's lap. If you are to sit here, make yourself worthy first of all."

Suniti was shocked to hear these words. Her heart felt the pangs of pain. Humiliation smote her like a dagger. She had been bearing with this insult and injustice since that day when Suruchi had enticed the King to expel her out of the palace. She had been leading the life of a *sannaysin* in the forest since that day. She did not pine for the comfortable life of a queen but she could not tolerate her son languishing in poverty. Being the eldest son of the king, he was entitled to a prince's honourable life. But he was called 'a beggar's son' and expelled from his kingdom. This incident reminded her again of all the previous insults. 'How could Suruchi hurt the soft heart of this godly child?' this thought almost killed her.

As her eyes met the child's, he asked, "Mother, why are you so quiet? Why don't you say something to me?"

Suniti was moved to tears. She patted her child's anguished face and replied – "Dhruv dear, why do you weep? What is great to sit on the throne of the King? Why do you grieve for being pushed down from your father's lap? You can sit in the lap of the King of the kings".

"Are you speaking the truth, mother?" Dhruv's face brightened up as he asked the question.

Looking at his smiling face, she said, "Yes Dhruv, there is God's throne which is far superior to the King's. God is the mightiest Emperor of the whole universe. You can get that throne if you worship God with a true heart."

"Mother, where would I find God?"

"He lives in each nook and corner of the universe. He is present in your heart too. You are to call Him with a loving heart and He would come to meet you." As Suniti spoke about the grace of God, she forgot her sorrow and looked blissful. Dhruv gazed at his mother's joyous face. Then, he got down from her lap and said, "Then, bless me mother, I am leaving to find God."

"What?" Suniti's heart missed a beat. "What are you saying Dhruv? You are just a child of five years. How can you follow the hard path of prayer in the forest? No! son, first grow up, then follow this path of penance."

"No, mother! I must go now. I must achieve that highest throne by God's grace. I will go just now."

His words and face spoke of his determination. Mother knew her child's strong mind. She understood that he had made up his mind and no obstacle could stop him now. Though a child of five, the power of his courage and conviction defied his age.

Suniti believed in his commitment to God and kissing his forehead blessed him, "Go my dear son! My blessings are always with you. Never be afraid of anyone in the forest because God will save you from all troubles. Go and achieve your goal."

His prayers were heard by God. When he returned after six months, his godly face glowed with inner knowledge. He had learnt at the feet of Devrishi Narada in the forest and realised God at such a young age. That is why his name Dhruv has become synonymous of 'the determined one.' And shines eternal as a star in the sky.

In the history of mankind this was an only incident - the youngest sanyasin to go in search of God.

□

Committed to Truth

She reached the funeral ground weeping bitterly. Clutching her dead son to her breast, wearing dirty sari, she looked like an image of sorrow. As she looked around the horrible place, the thought of putting her dear son on that cursed earth, made her unconscious with grief. After coming to senses, she wailed – "Ah! My darling prince, without you I am left alone...exiled from our kingdom, separated from my husband...and now my last support my son Rohit..."

As she called his name, the man in the funeral ground stopped abruptly. He was the servant of a pariah of the funeral-ground who charged tax from every person. 'Rohit' word struck him like thunderbolt. He rushed towards her and gazed at her face. Recognising her he cried piteously – 'Ah! It is you Shaiveya and this is our son Rohit! Oh: God!' He fell crest fallen on the ground. Recognising her husband, she clung to him. Both wept bitterly as if earth and the sky were joined in a sea of tears.

He was King Harishchander of Ayodhaya and she was her wife Shaiveya. Their ill-luck started on the day when Harishchander gave away his kingdom as a fulfilment of a vow to sage Vishwamiter. The sage wanted to test his commitment to truth. Therefore the king went through many hardships. He left his kingdom with his wife and son like an ordinary person. They had to sell themselves as servants. So Shaiveya sold herself to a lady while Harishchandera sold himself to a pariah. This amount was given to the Rishi Vishwamiter as Dakshina. Even this calamity did not waiver them in their resolve to follow the path of truth. Working as a pariaha's servant could not weaken his heart. He accepted it as a test of his patience and commitment to truth. Shaiveya, too, braved all hardships while doing all kinds of menial jobs for her mistress. But when her son was bitten by snake, she lost all patience. It was too much for her tolerance. Now she had brought him to the funeral ground.

After a while Harishchander regained control of his feelings and remembered his duty. He said, "Shaiveya, you have to pay the tax for the coffin of the dead body."

She looked at him in a daze as if asking – "A father demanding tax for his son's coffin?" It was the hardest, the cruellest moment of their life.

"Yes, Sheviya, I have to charge tax because it is my duty." She understood her husband's helplessness. But like a true wife she did not let him down. She controlled her heart and with inhuman courage laid her son on the ground. Then she tore away half of her Sari and wrapped her son in that coffin. Now she had no need to give money for it. As she placed the child in her husband's hands, both trembled at heart and the whole universe, too, was shaken to the core. Suddenly Vishwamitar came there – "Enough...enough now! Blessed be your name Harishchandera and Shaiveya! Blessed is your sacrifice for Truth. You have come out successful just as gold from the fire." With these words Rishi Vishwamitar embraced both. He treated the child with herbs and brought him back to life. Then, he handed over the kingdom of Ayodhaya with his blessings to Satyavadi Harishchander.

□

Ratna

The rains have come
Pea-cocks dance in the forests
Swings are on the trees
And I miss my parents, village
Where friends enjoying swings
Are feeling heavenly bliss

Ratna's lips were singing this song while she sat at her door-step alone. It was rainy season. She imagined her friends back from their husband's home...enjoying the swings on trees while singing and having fun. Mother would be cooking Malpooas in the kitchen and her brother, sister must be missing her as she is missing them. This thought made her burst into tears. Today she longed to go to her parent's house. She had not been there since long. After marriage her husband did not let her go anywhere. He was so obsessed with his pretty wife that even a day's absence was not acceptable to him. Ratna, too, loved her husband very much. But how could she forget the love of her parental home? She longed to go there and meet all. She had asked her husband to send her only for a few days to enjoy the rainy season at her parents. But he always refused with this question – “And what will become of me without you? You are my Ratna – the jewel.”

Today she felt very sad. She felt as if her parental home was calling her...and just then, someone called – “Ratna Didi....” She started...it was her brother ! She got up to meet him – “Oh ! how I missed you dear brother!” She spoke amid sobs.

He wiped her tears and said, “We all have missed you Didi. That's why I am here. Mother told me – “I won't let you enter the home without Ratna.”

At this she laughed like a little girl. In no time, she got ready to go. Her husband being away, she wrote a letter and put it under the pillow.

** ** ** ** ** **

It was quite dark at night when he reached home. He was surprised not to find Ratna at the door as usual. She must be in the kitchen – he went in but did not find her. Then he looked for her in other rooms but she was no where. “Where could she go?” Suddenly the paper under the pillow caught his eye. He read it - “Oh, gone to her parent's home.” He fell on the bed like one who had lost everything. He moaned in sorrow, “What is left for me here without her? No, I cannot live without my Ratna. I will go and bring her back...” This thought propelled him to rise and go out.

It was pitch dark with the black clouds raining heavily. He stumbled with stones on the muddy way. But no rain could stop him. He reached the stream. His in-laws house lay across the stream. He looked for a boat. But at this late hour with rainfall, no boat was there. The menacing river stood challenging him. But no challenge could beat him today. He jumped into the river. He chanced to get hold of a dead body floating by. So he swam through the river holding it.

Soon he was at the threshold of his in laws house. The door of the house was closed. Only one light glimmered from the window of the room upstairs. It was Ratna’s room. He smiled to himself – “Ratna must be waiting for me.”

But how to reach her? The door being closed, he had to climb the wall only. But how to climb without holding any support? Suddenly he saw a rope hanging from the window. He quickly caught it with both hands and reached the window. Now he jumped into the room. There she was – sleeping peacefully!. He rushed to her side and passionately called – "Ratna...Ratna...my dear...see, I have come."

She woke up with a start. Her eyes opened wide..."Who was he? Was it her husband ?" She got up immediately. Wonder-struck she asked – "You? How did you reach here?" The rain? The stream and...?' He replied in a jubilant voice – "Oh, it was nothing...I crossed the river holding on to a dead-body...and climbed the wall holding the rope you had hung outside the window..."

"A rope outside the window"...hearing these words, she ran to the window and shrieked in panic...there was a big snake hanging on the wall! She was horrified at the mad frenzy with which he had travelled to reach her.

"Oh, my God" she was grief-stricken. Looking him into the eyes she spoke in disgust – "The great passion that drove you to risk your life just to be with me – a body of flesh and bones – if only you had put that love and effort to find Lord Rama, you could have found him who is the real Ratna (jewel)."

The words struck him like thunder. The bare truth unveiled his eyes like lightning. Now nothing existed before him not even Ratna – he turned back swiftly and went the way he had come. After years of penance in the forest, from that love-lorn youth was born the great poet Tulsidas who wrote the famous epic *The Ram Charit Manas.*

□

A Celestial Singer

A fourteen year old girl was narrating her dream to her mother by singing thus;

Maain Mahane supane bari Gopal,
Raati peeti chunari odhi mehandi haath rasaal

(Mother, I saw Gopal Krishna coming to marry me. I was wearing the bridal-dress made of red and gold yarn.)

Mother laughed over her dream and said – "You are really mad, dear. How can Lord Krishan come to marry you? Dreams are dreams and these cannot be real." She silenced the girl for the time being but she knew at heart that Meera had been made for Krishna since her early childhood. She was a rare child born with two gifts. One was the gift of singing her own songs and the other was her deep love for Krishan. She used to play with the idol of Krishna as her companion and sing songs of love. These songs came natural to her like the nightingale. She kept singing while playing with Krishna whom she called her beloved.

As mother remembered Meera's childhood, she felt worried for this madness. Because tomorrow her marriage was to take place. Prince Bhoj Raj Sisodiya of Mewar was coming to wed

Meera. He had also heard many tales about Meera's love for Krishna. But he did not expect this when he saw an idol of Krishna kept beside his seat in the *Marriage-mandap*. He was more surprised when Meera held the idol in her hands while performing seven rounds of marriage. In fact, she married not only Bhoj Raj but Krishna too before the holy fire.

After the wedding her friends asked in jest, "Meera, what were you doing in the Mandap? you were marrying two persons – Kunwar Bhoj Raj and Krishna?"

But Meera replied seriously in a song –

Aise var ko ke varun jo janme aur mar Jai
Var variye Gopal ji maharo chudalo amar ho jai.

(Why marry such husband who is born and dies someday? I have married Gopal Krishna who is always with me from – birth to death).

When mother was preparing for her departure from home, Meera implored her to give her beloved Krishna's idol to take with her. Meera received a royal welcome and appreciation at her in-laws Palace. Her beauty and sweet voice won everybody's heart.

But one day her mother-in-law was displeased with her because when she told her to perform Gauri-Puja like other brides, Meera refused to do it. She replied in a song –

Mero to Girdhar gopal Dusaro na koi
Jake sir mor mukat mero pati soi

(I have none other than my Gopala. I worship none except him who has pea-cock feather on his head – only he is my husband.)

Hearing this all were shocked. Even Bhoj Raj felt pained at her wife's words. But he understood her deep love for Lord Krishna. So he accepted her as she was and did not expect her to be his wife. He got a temple of Ranchhor Krishna constructed in her palace. Bhoj Raj was married to another girl. Now Meera was totally immersed in worshipping and singing in her temple. By that time her songs of Krishna had become so popular that they were on everybody's lips. After five years of marriage, Bhoj Raj died suddenly. Now a widow, Meera became a target of her in-laws who objected to her singing and dancing in Krishna's temple. According to the orthodox rules of society, dancing and singing was blasphemous. Everyone criticised her for this. None could understand her pure heart which was full of love for Lord Krishna. Her brother-in-law Kunwar Vikramjeet was very harsh to her. He tried to kill her by giving her poison in the name of Krishna's holy water. Meera drank it in good faith. And Lo! She survived the poison ! But he tried again and sent a snake in a basket in the name of Shaligram (Krishna's idol). Meera was quick to open it and a miracle happened. In place of the snake, there was Krishna's idol in the basket. Meera embraced it happily. Lord Krishna was indeed with her defending from all misfortunes. But this torture was too much for Meera. She felt like a bird in a cage. She yearned for freedom. She fell sick. When doctor was called to treat her, she said in a song –

Babul vaid bulaiya re pakari dhikhai mahari bahan
Jav vaid ghar aapne re yeh dukh tumaro nah

(No doctor can heal me because he knows not the cause of my illness.)

Only Meera could heal herself. So one day she left the palace which had imprisoned her free soul and went to Vrinda Van - the city where Krishna was born. After travelling on foot like a pilgrim, singing and dancing in groups, she reached Krishna's temple. But the priest refused her to enter as he had never allowed any woman to worship the Lord. On hearing his words, Meera laughed heartily and asked him, "As far as I know there is only one man on Earth who is my Gopal Krishna in this temple. I wonder if there is another man too?"

The priest understood the hidden meaning of her words. He was ashamed of his audacity to prohibit a true worshipper of Lord Krishna. He bowed before her and let her in. Meera stood before the smiling Gopal Krishna and felt immense joy. She stood gazing at her beloved – her heart filled with heavenly bliss, her eyes full of tears, her lips whispering notes of love. The idol seemed to come to life. Meera heard Krishna calling her and she fell down in ecstasy. Meera left her body and became one with her love, Lord Krishna. Meera's songs are being sung everyday and they are our eternal heritage.

□

Devki

It was pitch dark. The prison was also drowned in darkness. The eerie silence of one prison-room was broken by sound of sobs. A dim lamp showed two persons – Devki and Vasudev – the couple had been suffering here since their wedding day.

Devki was sobbing while the memories of past pained her. She remembered the day of her wedding. How fortunate she was to be married to such a noble man as Vasudev. She, too, was daughter of Ugarsen, king of Mathura. Her brother Kansa was the crown prince. He was taking her to her in-law's house on his royal chariot. She deemed herself the luckiest one at that moment. On way Devki tried to advise her brother sweetly – "Dear Brother, I am going away leaving father in your care. He is old and you are the crown-prince. So it is your responsibility to see that the state is ruled with justice and kindness. But I am pained to see that people suffer due to your ways of injustice and..." Her words were interrupted by Kansa's shouting..."Stop it, Devki. How dare you advise me how to rule my people?" He flew into a violent fit of anger and tried to throw her down the chariot.

Devki was too shocked to do anything. It was Vasudev who came forward and begged Kansa to pardon his sister. Devki wept bitterly. But Kansa showed his true colours. He could not tolerate his critic - may be his own sister. He was used to crush any voice of dissent. So poor Devki and Vasudev were taken to the prison instead of their sweet home. That was how the newly wed couple started their life in the dark prison-cell. It was then that Devki pledged to give birth to a son who will punish Kansa for his sins.

But destiny was cruel enough for her. She remembered that auspicious hour when she gave birth to a son. Both were holding the newly born with happiness. Devki said - "God is so gracious to listen to my prayer. My son will fulfil my wish and save the people from cruel Kansa." But words were still in her mouth, when Kansa entered like a Devil. He snatched the baby from her arms and laughed loudly – "Your son will save the people if he himself is saved by me." Sensing his cruelty, both fell on their knees and begged for their son's life. But Kansa went away and killed the child by throwing it on a stone.

Devki trembled with that painful memory. That tragedy occurred again when her second son was born. They suffered this unbearable torture seven times. Now the eighth baby was to be born and this was their last hope. Both were worried to death. Kansa grew a bigger monster with each killing. When his father tried to advise him, he put him too in prison. They wanted to save this son for their redemption. So Vasudev thought of a clever plan. He manipulated a prison-officer to open the door at midnight so that the child may be taken out. According to the plan, as soon as Devki gave birth to a son, Vasudev put it in a basket and went out.

The dark night had turned darker with torrential rain. Vasudev advanced towards river Yamuna. It was very difficult to wade through it but with rare courage and God's strength, he succeeded in crossing it safely. He rushed to Nand's house in Gokul. As planned with him, he was to exchange his son with Yashodha's daughter. This was done quickly and he returned to the prison before dawn. None came to know of all this drama which destiny had helped to be played.

As the sun rose, Kansa came to know of the birth of Devki's eighth son for whom he had heard many astrologers' predictions. He hurried to kill this boy who might be a danger to his life. When he saw a girl, he laughed like a devil - "A mere girl to be a danger to the mighty Kansa. That proves how foolish and useless are all the predictions!"

As he was taking away the baby to kill, Devki smiled in her heart and said in whisper – "Foolish Kansa ! You will never know that our saviour is safe in Yashoda's arms. Now you count your days. You will be punished well by our Saviour."

With a heart full of contentment, Devki thought of her Godly son whose bright face was to dispel all darkness from their lives. And time proved her right. As Krishna grew up and killed Kansa, all heaved a sigh of relief. Ugarsen was released from prison and enthroned by Krishna. People were released from Kansa's tyrannical rule and Devki Vasudev saw the light of the day in freedom after years of imprisonment. When Krishna stood before his mother and called 'Ma', Devki felt immensely pleased. Overwhelmed with love, she uttered these words – "Krishna, you are not only my son but the saviour for all".

□

Yashoda Maiyya

"Nand Rani Yashoda Maiyya has been blessed with a son who is beautiful and dark like a "Neelmani (blue sapphire)". The whole village of Brij Bhoomi was agog with this news. All young and old ladies rushed to Yashoda's house as she was dear to all. They were excited and joyous with the arrival of her first son after years of wait. All felt as if not only Yashoda but everyone has been blessed. Songs from their smiling lips filled the air with fragrance of love.

As Yashoda gazed at the lovely baby she forgot all pain - even that pain which she felt while giving away her new-born daughter to Vasudeva. When he approached them at midnight with his new born son and a request to exchange him with her daughter, she knew that it would be killed by King Kansa of Mathura. But when Vasudeva implored her – "Sister, you will save not only my son but a saviour for the people too." Then she replied sweetly – "Tell my sister Devki that her son is safe with me and I will bring him up as his mother."

'Neelmani' was the name she had fondly given to her son. But the baby was so attractive that everyone who saw his lovely face, called him with a new name. So there sprang up a lot of names like Shyam, Sanwara, Krishana, Kanihaya, Murli-Manohar etc. Yashoda's house was always full of neighbours who wanted to have a look at her darling Neelmani. She did special pooja to ward off any ill-will towards him. Looking at his chubby face and bright eyes, she imagined the day when he will call her 'Maiyya' (Ma). She dreamed how he would learn to walk, ask for butter or steal it from the kitchen. And all those dreams started becoming real when Krishna grew up to be the naughtiest boy of Brij Bhoomi. He started his day with stealing butter from all kitchens along with his friends. So he was called Makhan-chor (Butter-thief) by all.

One day he shocked all, when he stopped ladies who were taking pitchers of milk and butter to Mathura. As Yashoda admonished him saying – "O, Neelmani, what are you doing? You are inviting trouble for us. Don't stop this everyday practice of sending milk and butter for the king."

"No, Maiyya," the young boy replied in anger, "This milk and butter is earned with our sweat, so it belongs to us only. Now the tyrant Kansa won't ever get it, come what may."

With these words little Krishna challenged the might of Kansa. But now it was imperative to be prepared for the outcome. So Krishna became the leader of all young boys and started to learn the art of wrestling, archery, sword-fight etc. They learnt these from Sandipani Guru at his Ashram nearby. All this preparation went on secretly. Krishna was too clever to let Yashoda come to know of it. Whenever she instructed Krishna – "Kanha, be careful of strangers in the forest. Kansa's agents are always after you and beware of that mighty *Naag* (snake) that lives in the Yamuna River."

Then naughty Krishna, wore an innocent look and replied sweetly – "No, Maiyya, I neither go near Yamuna nor to the forest alone. Do not worry for me. Ma."

But can a luminary like Krishna ever remain hidden? Each

day brought a new incident that proved Krishna's courage and wisdom. When faced with Shaktasur, Pootna, Bakasur, Kaaliya Naag, Keshi etc. Krishna proved his extraordinary strength and intelligence. Yashoda's heart swelled with pride on hearing his son's feats of courage but her motherly feelings got disturbed with worry.

** ** ** ** ** **

Eleven years passed like eleven hours. Yashoda's sweet dream was broken when Akroor's chariot from Mathura reached there to take away Krishna. She could not believe her eyes that her 'Neelmani' was to leave by that chariot. Her tear-bedimmed eyes could not bear to see her 'Maakhan-Chor' leave her...Krishna had become her very soul, not only her but of all the people. He had become their dearest son, friend and saviour too. No one could bear to send him away to Mathura.

Yashoda held her 'Neelmani' in her embrace...her eyes shedding tears, lips muttering –"No, I won't let my Krishna go anywhere" and she clasped him tightly in her arms. Akroor stood helplessly. None could force Yashoda to let go of Krishna. At last, Krishna raised his head and spoke softly, "Maiyya, let me go. I swear by you that I will come back to you after killing the tyrant Kansa."

Kansa's name was enough to remind Yashoda of a promise she had made to Vasudeva on that night of Krishna's arrival. As those memories rushed to her mind, she realised the truth that Krishna was not her son. He had come to her as a blessing, a heavenly boon for some years. She was only a trustee of that treasure which belonged to Devki and to the people for whom he was the Saviour. She now remembered Vasudeva's words – "He is not only our son but a Saviour of the people from Kansa."

Now she let go of Krishna from her embrace. Then all gave Krishna a tearful farewell. After sometime when news of 'killing of Kansa by Krishna' reached Yashoda, she smiled through her tears. As years went by and Krishna grew up to become the King of Dwarka , Architect of the Great War of Mahabharata, Yogi Raj Preacher of Gita – sitting on the high pedestal of fame and glory, Krishna always felt the sweet warmth of affection of Yashoda Maiyya in his heart.

□

The Blind Affection

"Dear daughter, these are from your in-laws," adorning her pretty daughter with glittering ornaments and clothes, mother could not hold back her tears.

After she left, her daughter was quick to ask from a friend – "Why is mother weeping so bitterly? Is it due to my engagement? Does she grieve for my departure?"

"No, Gandhari, it is not due to your departure, it is to grieve for your engagement with the prince of Hastinapur Dhritrashtra." Her friend explained.

"But, what of that? Is not the prince good and handsome?"

"The prince is a noble, handsome youngman – but blind by birth."

As she completed the sentence, Gandhari felt like falling from the skies. Her maiden's dreams of love and marriage were shattered to pieces. Within a moment her bright world turned pitch dark. She sat motionless like a statue. Now she understood the cause of her mother's tears. The thought of her dark future brought a sea of tears in her beautiful eyes.

After a while she took one piece of cotton cloth and placing it over her eyes, tightened it like a bandage. Seeing this, her friends shouted in horror – "Gandhari, what is this? Why have you covered your eyes with this bandage?"

Hearing this horrible news, mother came running – "Daughter, open this bandage...do not cover these beautiful eyes..." mother tried to remove her bandage weeping bitterly.

"No, mother," Gandhari put away mother's hands from her eyes and said strongly. "I have to become worthy of my life partner. I won't accept that happiness which is denied to him. This is what you have taught me, mother. Bless me to be true to your teaching."

Gandhari's resolute step could not be retraced by her father, mother, relatives or friends. All stood helpless as the beautiful princess was sent to Hastinapur to be married with Dhritrashtra. It was a forced marriage as Bhisham Pitahmah had forced King Subal of Gandhar to marry his daughter with the blind prince with the threat of battle on refusal. So Gandhari's fate was sealed on that day.

** ** ** ** ** **

Gandhari stood at the roof of her palace. She could hear the chirping of birds and know that it was dawn. She wore a worried look. Her heart was heavy with grief. Deep sighs heaved her breast. It was the 1st day of the great war of Mahabharata. Her mind was in turmoil. Memories of bygone days came to her mind and each memory aggravated her agony. She had never been so grief-stricken as today. Her conscience pricked her and whispered in her ears – "It is you and you alone who is responsible for this war." She could hear the wise Vidur tell her on her first son Duryodhana's birth – "This son of yours will be the root cause for the annihilation of your whole clan." But she became really blind to all advice. She neither gave up that son nor kept a strong check on his activities. Taking advantage of his parents' blindness, their son grew to be the ring-leader of all other ninety-nine brothers. They indulged in all kinds of deceit, hooliganism, injustice and torture to the people. They were specially tyrants for the gentle Pandavas who were their cousin-brothers.

"Ah, if only I had opened my eyes and removed my bandage and seen for myself how my son was becoming a tyrant: I could have snubbed him in the beginning. Oh ! My closed eyes and blind affection are responsible for that vicious seed of hatred which grew into a strong tree of war. I am responsible for this Mahabharata. Look at another mother Kunti – a helpless widow with five sons. It was due to her wise and strict guidance that her sons grew up as warriors possessing the best qualities of men. And I proved an utter failure, though a queen." Tears streamed from her closed eyes.

"Ma, I offer my salutations to you. Bless me," these words brought her back from past.

"Who is there? Is it Duryodhana?" Gandhari asked recognising the voice of his son.

"Yes, mother, it is – your son. Today is the first day of Mahabharata and I have come for your blessings. Bless me with victory."

Gandhari kept quiet for a while. Her heart felt the pang of pain. She knew her son begged for her blessings. But her conscience could not bless him with victory. She replied..."Son, victory will bless the righteous one." For eighteen days her son came to have her blessings for victory in the war. Each day his voice grew weaker but mother repeated the same reply – "Where there is Dharma, there is victory." She knew at heart that her son craved for her blessings and this would inspire him to victory. But now she did not wish to succumb to that blind affection which was responsible to turn him into such a tyrant. She wanted to atone for her irresponsible motherhood. She could not bless her wicked son to win the war.

As Mahabharat ended annihilating all Kauravas, the wails and tears of her widowed daughters-in-law shook Gandhari's heart. She lost her courage, her forbearance, her patience. As she stood before Krishna in the battlefield, she uttered these words sobbing- "Keshav, it is not the Kauravas, but mother of Kauravas, who is defeated in this War. It is a defeat of that mother who had herself shut her eyes from the responsibility to give good education to her sons. And it is the victory of Mother Kunti who though widow and penniless, was alert and responsible enough to bring up her sons in a very ideal way. I admit my blunder – father being born blind, mother deliberately turned blind to be true to her husband. But both shirked their duties as good parents. Both had blind affection that favoured their sons to become tyrants. That is why my hundred sons fell like sand-forts before the formidable five sons of Kunti. It is the victory of good breeding over bad breeding by parents."

□

A Responsible Mother

When King Pandu died while living in the forest, his queen Kunti got ready to end her life by burning herself with her husband. As the funeral-fire was lit, the younger queen Maadri held her weeping bitterly – "No, you must not leave me, dear sister. Though being elder, you have the right to be 'Sati', still I implore you to grant me this right. I am younger to you not only in age but ability too. So if you remain alive, you will bring up our sons in a better way. So please, accept my request and let our fatherless sons have a good mother."

Kunti was a very wise woman. She saw the truth in Maadri's words. So controlling her emotions, she got down from the funeral pyre and let Maadri be burnt with her husband. With a heart heavy with the loss of her husband and sister, she returned to her ashram.

"Where is father Ma? We don't see Chhoti Ma with you?" her sons encircled her anxiously.

Kunti embraced all and wiping her tears said, "Sons, your father and Chhoti Ma left for their heavenly abode. They have left you in my care. Now you have only me as your father and mother," and they all burst into tears. This pathetic sight made everyone at the Ashram cry with them.

Daughter of King Kunt, wife of king Pandu, mother of five sons, was today a lonely widow who had neither her husband nor her kingdom. King Pandu had renounced his kingdom and come to live in the forest. But now she could not go on living like this. She had to protect and educate her sons like Kshatriya princes. So she decided to return to her kingdom. If God had given her this responsibility, she must discharge it in the best way.

Kunti was escorted by other hermits of the Ashram to the palace of Dhritrashtra – the blind brother of Pandu who was reigning in his place. The king gave her a separate palace and got her sons admitted to the royal school. But as days passed, Kunti experienced that life here was more a bed of thorns for her sons specially. As they studied with Kaurava brothers, they suffered all kinds of humiliation and torture. Duryodhana was the ring leader to inflict this specially on Bheema and Arjuna. He was always devising schemes to end their lives. So Kunti always feared for their safe return in the evening.

One day they did not come till late in the evening. Kunti stood at the door fearing the worst. At last she saw them coming. But they were holding Bheema by the shoulders and their faces were flushed with anger. As they came near, Bheem thundered in fury – "Look at me Ma! That cursed devil Duryodhana made me drink seeds of poppy and then threw me down into the river. It was by the grace of God that I came to my senses and swam out alive otherwise you could never see your son alive..."

"Don't utter such words my dear," Kunti embraced him weeping. "Ah! How hard is destiny on us!"

"But I won't return home till I have broken that proud head with my 'Mace'" with these words Bheema got up abruptly and ran out of the palace. All stood rooted to the ground. But Kunti was quick to run after him and hold him fast – "No, Bheema" she spoke strongly, "No, my son, you won't do this. I know you are strong enough to punish him. But this is not the proper time to do this. Time will come when you will fight them with your mighty weapon 'Mace.' But now we have to fight them with the power of wisdom. When you are fully educated and well-versed in warfare, you will challenge them with a superior power and win back your right to rule the kingdom that belonged to your late father."

Mother's words of wisdom worked like soothing balm over their sore hearts. They were intelligent enough to understand them, though this happened not once but again and again. They had to eat an humble pie at the hands of tyrant Kauravas. At that time, it was very difficult to restrain Bheema and Arjuna to punish them. But they were always controlled by mother's strong words – "Not now," and the ideal sons could never think to disobey their mother.

Time passed but the tyranny of Kauravas did not stop. Though Pandavas were able to regain their lost kingdom with mother's wisdom and their own superior strength, still the crooked Duryodhana hatched a sinister plan and snatched their kingdom in a game of *Chauser*. After an exile of thirteen years, Pandavas came back and asked Dhritrashtra to give back their kingdom as they had now the right to claim it. But all attempts by the elder men, including Lord Krishna could not succeed in getting back their kingdom. Then Yudhishtra sent an offer through Krishna that they would accept even five villages from them. But Duryodhana refused point-blank and said – "Five villages? No, I won't give even an inch of land without fighting a war."

When this news reached Kunti, her old and frail body shook like a tree in tempest. Like a tigress she thundered – "Krishna, I am ashamed of my eldest son's cowardice. Tell him to stop this parrot-like repetition of peace and Dharama. Religion does not make a man coward and peace is not to be begged. Peace is won through war only. Tell Yudhistra to be a man and not a beggar before a tyrant. Let him remember that I gave birth to a Kshatriya and educated him to manifest his manhood. Does not he feel ashamed of his cowardice to leave his mother at the mercy of others?"

These hard hitting words ignited the fire out of his weak heart and plunged him into the great war of Mahabharata. With the full support of his brothers and Krishna he succeeded in the total annihilation of the Kauravas and victory of Pandạvas.

When Yudhishtra sat on the throne of Hastinapur along with his wife and brothers, his mother heaved a sigh of relief and blessed them.

Now was the time to enjoy a life of contentment and luxury but for Kunti it was the hour of renouncing all. She decided to accompany old Dhritrashtra and Gandhari to live in the forests. When her sons implored her to stay, she replied strongly - "As a mother it was my duty to educate and prepare you for a life you were meant to have as king. Now I am content to go to the forest and lead my life in prayer and service."

□

Rose in Thorns

In Ashok-Vatika Sita sat under the Ashoka-tree. Though the garden was full of trees and flowers, yet they were devoid of soothing softness and fragrance. As armed guards stood behind the trees, these, too, looked sinister like the guards. The flowers had lost their lovely sweetness with the presence of demon-women around them. Sita never looked at anything. Her beautiful face had the pallor of grief, her luminous eyes looked like pools of tears, and her silken tresses bound in a plait looked dull and forlorn like her. She looked like a withered rose surrounded by thorns.

As night fell, everything was plunged into darkness. An eerie silence prevailed every where. Even the guards could not remain awake. But Sita's eyes knew no sleep. How could she sleep? Images of her bygone days filled her eyes. She was lost in those memories which were her only companions in this friendless land.

First image was of Janakpuri – her parental home. She saw vivid pictures of those moments of excitement, when encircled with friends, she had gone to the temple for Gauri-Puja. And the ecstasy she felt when she saw prince Ram and Laxman there. Even now she experienced that strange sensation of deep love that lives on till now. Then, those hard moments of anxiety before Rama broke the celestial Bow and she put garland around his handsome face. Ah! What a royal welcome she, along with her sisters, received at Ayodhya...that warm embrace by Mother Kaushlaya, Sumitra and Kaikeyi. But those days of love and luxury passed soon like moments and she was hit by the news of exile to Rama into the forest for fourteen years. Rama insisted Sita not to accompany him. How could she, being a princess, bear the difficult life of forests? But Sita gave up her life of luxury and comfort in a moment. Her strong words were, "In sorrow or joy, palace or forest, my place is always with you." She made a choice to walk on the thorny path with her beloved because the path might be full of thorns but her heart was filled with flowers of love. She had the bliss of being with her husband. When she cooked, cleaned and worked in the hut, she forgot the comforts of palace. She felt like a free bird, singing and roaming in the forest with Rama.

"Ah! those golden days disappeared soon...and now I am imprisoned here by that devil Ravana who abducted me in that false guise of a saint!" This bitter memory shook Sita with anger. Her helplessness brought tears in her eyes. She looked up and spoke, "O Ashoka tree! Your name means reliever of sorrow! Why don't you relieve me of my sorrow? I can no more live this cursed life without Rama. Ah! those moments of humiliation and torture when Ravana comes to lure or threaten me? Oh, Ashoka tree relieve me of this torture? Your leaves shine like sparks of fire. Drop one for me so that I may be burnt alive."

As she waited, something dropped from the tree. She was startled. "Has Ashoka listened to my entreaty"? She looked around – something shone on the earth.

It was a ring. As she took it in her hand, her heart missed a beat. She gasped in fear. "It is Rama's ring! How did it come to this enemy land? Who brought it? How? Did he snatch it...?" She could not think further. Her heart trembled. The thought of Ram's safety distressed her.

"Mother, this servant of Rama bows to your feet." These words gave her another shock. She was surprised to see a small monkey-man before her. She stepped back in fear.... "Is it some other farce of Ravana?"

Sensing her doubt, he again bowed and spoke gently, "Mother, believe me, I am Hanuman – a messenger of Sri Rama. I have been given this ring by Sri Rama himself to give to you as a proof." Then he narrated some incidents told to him by Rama so that Sita might believe him. Now Sita had faith in him. She was overwhelmed with Rama's love for her. Her whole sorrow of separation vanished and she hugged Rama's ring to her heart and wept.

Seeing this Hanuman was also moved to tears. He requested, "Mother, your life and honour is in danger here. If you permit me, I can carry you on my back and fly to Sri Rama's place."

These words electrified Sita's heart into rapture. She would be free from Ravana's prison and be with her dear Rama – this thought enlightened her dark life.

"Please, permit me, mother!" Hanuman repeated his request. Sita started at his words. All of a sudden her mind got cleared from the mist of emotions. She realised the full implication of this. Controlling her feelings, she gave a cool thought to it and replied strongly – "No, Hanuman. Your request comes out of your heart full of genuine concern for me. But I do not want to go like this. It is honourable neither for me nor for my husband. It would be worthy for a Kshatriya warrior like Rama to challenge Ravana in a war and punish him. He should free me from this prison and take away with him. Go and convey this message to my Rama."

Thus Sita showed exemplary courage and power of conviction as she made this choice. Her whole life – from birth to death proved this. In her long span of life, there were only short spans of joy or comfort. Because whenever there was a choice between life of honour or comfort, she chose the first. It culminated in the last span of her life when Rama was forced to send her away to live in the forest at Valmiki's Ashram. She lived there with a head held high and gave birth to two sons. She fulfilled the responsibility of a good mother. After getting them grown up and educated, she sent them to their father. But again, she had the same choice when she was asked to give proof for her purity by fire and now she chose to embrace death than bow to another test. She was a rose whose destiny was written with thorns but its fragrance fills the land eternally.

□

The Forgotten One

When Sumant's chariot carried away Ram, Sita and Laxman to the forest for exile of fourteen years, every man, woman and child of Ayodhaya including the royal family ran after it. But the speeding chariot disappeared in no time. Now all came back weeping. Everyone talked about their great sacrifice and sympathised with the royal family.

But no one cared to look to a corner of the palace, where someone was shedding silent tears. No eye shed a tear for her; no lip had a word of praise for her sacrifice.

This forgotten one was Urmila – Laxman's wife. Standing behind a window, she was gazing at the distant path on which the chariot had disappeared a moment ago. She was struggling hard to control her violent rush of tears. Her heart asked again and again, "Why did you keep mum, when Laxman stood before you an hour ago?"

After Ram's resolve to go for exile to the forest, Sita had strongly expressed her desire to go with him. So when Laxman came to her with this news, "Bhaiyya Ram and Bhabhi Sita are leaving for the forest for fourteen years and I, too, am going with them for I can't live in Ayodhya without them"– last words choked his throat. His eyes were red with unshed tears. Urmila stood stunned. Her heart wanted to say, “Without you, Ayodhaya is unbearable for me. Take me along, dear.” But her lips could not express her desire. She wanted to say – “I won't come in the way of your duties there. When you will help your brother with your arrows and swords, I would share my sister's burden at home. Don't leave me in the prison of this palace for long fourteen years. Don’t deprive me of my right to be with my husband at this time.” But words could not come to her trembling lips and he could not read the language of her tear-bedimmed eyes.

So he went away saying – “I am going Urmila, You stay here and take care of grief-stricken father and mothers.”

Then Urmila found her tongue to say – “Aryaputar, rest assured I will take good care of them and wait for you” and she burst into uncontrollable tears. But he was gone by then.

After his return from the forest, Sumant, the charioteer, narrated in detail how Ram, Sita and Laxman put on the saffron robes, tied their silken hair into tight buns overhead, ate only fruit and vegetables and slept on bare earth. Urmila listened to everything and prepared to live like them. Her room looked like a hut now, bereft of furniture and other comforts. She discarded fine clothes and jewellery. She dressed like a sanaysin in saffron, ate only fruit and vegetables and slept on earth. When she appeared before her mothers-in-law, they all were shocked. They tried to change her mind but to no avail. She replied in sweet and strong words - “Mother, tell me, how can I enjoy that which is denied to him? Please, bless me to do this penance.” She devoted her whole time and energy in looking after them and discharging her duties for the royal family.

But when night fell and everyone went to sleep, her lonely heart would share her grief with the silent stars. She had only those moments for herself and only those companions to speak her mind. She would keep on waking and thinking – “Where can be my dear husband standing guard in the forest? Ah! I can't get any message from him! Why is destiny so cruel to me? Sister Sita has the fortune to be with her husband. Even sister Mandavi and Shrutkirti are with their husbands. Why is only Urmila's fate so sealed that she is deprived of even her beloved's message? How unfortunate is Urmila in the whole universe!"

One day she heard the news that prince Bharat and Shatrughan along with mothers were going to the forest to meet Rama at Chitrakoot. Everyone was excited and joyous to go and have a meeting with Rama but Urmila could not go with them. She did not ask for this and none could understand her heart to take her along. She kept behind like the worthy self-effacing daughter-in-law.

** ** ** ** ** **

When Hanuman passed over Ayodhaya while carrying Sanjiwani herb from the Himalayas to revive Laxman to life as he fell unconscious after being hit by Meghnaad, Urmila heard this bad news. She was shaken to the boots. Leaving aside her patience and modesty, she approached mother Sumitra and said courageously – "Mother, if you and Guruji allow me, I can lead an army to help Sri Rama in this war." Mother and Guru Vasisht were surprised at her courage. He praised her saying – "Daughter, Laxman cannot remain unconscious for long when his wife is so brave and inspiring. Your patience and devotion will act like his defensive armour and keep him safe." And it proved true when Laxman came back to life and won the war.

After fourteen years Ayodhaya woke up from the nightmare and was decorated like a bride to accord a royal welcome to the victorious Ram, Laxman and Sita. There were lights, flowers and music to welcome them home. Every man, woman and even the servants and pets of the palace received Ram, Sita and Laxman's loving words or touch of affection. But Urmila still waited in her room for her dear husband. Even now she was the last to receive her love of life.

□

Chhoti Ma

"Maharaniji, Brahamrishi Vasisht has come," when Manthara gave this message to Kaikeyi, she was engrossed in embroidering a silken shawl for Ram's coronation ceremony.

She went immediately to the door and brought him inside respectfully.

"Respected Guruji, what brings you here? Can I be of any service to you?" she asked with folded hands.

"Yes, Devi, I have come for some special service from you. I wish it won't trouble you."

"Trouble? No, Guruji, you are serving the people day and night and to obey you will be my good fortune. Please order me."

Vasisht kept thinking for a while. His calm face showed lines of worry. Then he spoke, "I have come to ask for a great sacrifice from the Maharani of Ayodhaya. You must be knowing that Ravana, the King of Lanka has brought death and destruction to the south of Bharat. Giant devils of his army are torturing hermits in the forests, kidnapping young girls from villages, looting valuables and killing innocent people everyday. The whole South is having a blood bath and cries of anguish fill the air." With these words Vasisht sighed in sorrow.

Kaikeyi, too, was moved to tears. She asked, "Maharishi, if you order me, I can command a large army and go to fight a war against Ravana's army." Vasisht remembered Kaikeyi had commanded an army to assist King Dashratha in a battle against Shambrasur. He knew she was a brave woman. "No, Maharani, you need not take to arms yourself, nor king Dushratha's soldiers can win this war."

"Then, who else can do it?"

"For this, only prince Rama..."

At Ram's name, Kaikeyi interrupted him with excitement, "Yes, Maharishi, it is Rama alone who can win this war. So you want me to get him ready for this. I will do this by convincing Ram's mother and father after the coronation. Rest assured," Saying this she heaved a sigh of relief.

But Maharishi did not seem relieved. He had the same worried look on his face. He took a long breath and spoke again, "Devi, you talk like the worthy queen of Raghukul. This encourages me to ask you for this sacrifice. I want you to ask for the award of those two boons which your husband had promised you in Shambrasur battle. For one boon, you are to ask for your son Bharat's coronation and for the second, for Rama's exile to the forests for fourteen years." As he completed the sentence, Kaikeyi felt like falling from the sky into the deepest ocean. She was too shocked to speak. Her senses were benumbed. Perplexed she looked towards him – "Was he serious or jesting?"

But his face was serious. Now she burst into tears and said, Maharishi, what are you telling me to do? Should I ask for my beloved son Rama's exile? You ask specially me to do this. Why me? It is I who had loved Rama the most. It is I whom Rama loves and respects the most. I have always loved Rama more than my Bharat. How can I send away such an able, loving and good son on exile for 14 years? How can I separate the newly wedded princess Sita from her dear husband?" With these words she felt as if her heart would break with unbearable grief.

Vasisht's eyes were also filled with tears. Controlling himself he said, "Devi, this is no doubt, the hardest decision and most cruel too, You and the whole family may suffer a lot due to this. But you are the Queen Mother for your people. Think of your greater responsibility towards the suffering men and women of Bharat. Don't fear for Rama's safety. He can accomplish this job successfully."

"But, what is the necessity for sending Ram into exile to accomplish this? I can prepare a large army and send Ram along with Bharat, Laxman and Shatrughan for the war."

"No, Maharani, this won't work. An army from Ayodhaya cannot defeat Ravana's forces spread all over the south. You cannot even imagine how strongly established is Ravan there ! We have come to this conclusion after a long consultations. Rama's exile of fourteen years is necessary to prepare an army of local tribals to challenge the enemy."

As the whole plan was explained to her she could not express her dissent. But her heart was in turmoil. She imagined the future—the anguish of Dashratha and Kaushlaya, protest from the people, everyone criticising and blaming her...and even her own heart...? She could think no more. With folded hands, she entreated again – "Maharishi, please change your plan a little. Don't burden me with such a big load of shame and guilt?"

"No, Maharani, Why do you think of guilt or shame? You are doing a great service to the suffering people. Your sacrifice will save the country. Remember, even Lord Mahadev accepted poison to give nectar to the world."

Now Vasisht got up to leave. Kaikeyi bowed to him. Before going, he explained the details of the plan to her.

As soon as he left, Kaikeyi pressed that golden embroidered shawl to her heart and said weeping – "Dear Ram, now your Chhoti Ma would offer you the saffron clothes instead of this golden shawl. From today 'Kaikeyi' word would become a synonym of 'Cruel step mother., After this, I will have to suffer all kinds of sorrow, guilt, shame, criticism and what not. But my dear Ram, do not misunderstand your Chhoti Ma. It is only you whom I trust, so don't stop loving me...let all blame me, let history record me as a cruel step-mother but you trust your unfortunate Chhoti Ma as I trust you my son."

And Rama did not betray her trust. He never doubted her love. He never stopped loving her as Chhoti Ma. That is why when he returned from exile, he first visited Kaikeyi's palace and addressed her lovingly – "Chhoti Ma !"

□

The Invincible Draupadi

The sky looked the colour of the earth in the evening. The battle-field of Kurukshetra had turned into a river of blood, where heads, arms, legs etc were rolling like pebbles in river. This had been the place where eighteen million soldiers had sacrificed their lives. Two clans of Hastinapura, the Kauravas and the Pandavas had fought a fierce war in which warriors from all over the country had participated. For eighteen days the war continued. At last the Pandavas won over the Kauravas. The victory cost dearly to Pandavas too. So even Pandavas felt the prick of pain.

The coronation ceremony of the eldest brother yudhishtra was to take place. Preparations were made, the priest had come. But yudhishtra sat gazing at the ground sighing. He showed no inclination to get up. His brothers waited in anguish.

Bheema and Arjuna tried again – "Brother, the priest tells us to hurry up, as the auspicious hour has come. The throne awaits the King."

"The King...?" Yudhishtra murmured like a defeated man "Whose King? There is no one left alive in this kingdom. For whom shall I ascend the throne?" His words were so cold that they sent a shiver to all. The victorious faces looked like the pale faces of the defeated. The winners of Mahabharata War hung their heads in sorrow.

But there was one person present who did not lower her head or eyes. She was Draupadi – the invincible wife of the Pandavas. Like a lightning, she got up, her beautiful face flushed, her eyes red with rage, her words came like sparks of fire, "*Aryaputar,* look at me – today there is none so unfortunate as I whose whole parental family is dead – whose five young sons were killed while sleeping at night! Just think of my loss! It is I who should mourn now and renounce the world." the memory of loved ones overwhelmed her and she wept bitterly.

All stood shaken with sorrow. Yudhishtra tried to console her saying, "That is why Draupadi, I feel guilty for your sorrow and want to renounce the crown..."

"No!" Draupadi interrupted him forcefully, "No, this is not the way to relieve my sorrow. You forget the real cause of my sorrow. How could you forget the day when we had to leave like beggars after losing everything at the hands of tyrant Duryodhana in that deceitful game of *chausar*? How could you forget my humiliation when those devils tried to disrobe me in the royal court? Have you forgotten those thirteen years of torture in the forests? Then, you used to pledge and plan with me to fight a decisive war with the Kauravas and win back our honour and kingdom. Now that everyone fought in Mahabharata and our efforts have borne fruit, you talk of renouncing the crown !" Draupadi's slender body shook in anger.

Yudhishtra again tried to justify himself –"Calm down Draupadi! just listen to me. When I think of sitting on the throne, my conscience pricks me – my heart trembles. I can't sit on this throne which is the outcome of this bloodshed ." And he hung his head in remorse.

But Draupadi could not do so. Her head held high, she roared like a lioness – "Dharam Raj ! Let not your eyes be blinded with the veil of false notions of conscience now. You have won a war defeating those who were tyrant rulers. Only a coward or a tyrant has no right to be a king. You are neither of the two. So like a real Khashtriya King it is your duty to rule the Kingdom. You should own your responsibility to give people a just and good rule. Talk of renunciation is a breach of trust to those who look to you for their well-being. Listen to the call of duty This is your Dharama now." Draupadi's stirring words injected a new life in Yudhishtra's body and soul. He realised his weakness and rose to the call of duty. With strong steps, he advanced towards the throne along with his invincible wife.

□

Re-Birth

As Savitri entered the royal court of King of Madra accompanied by senior ministers, all eyes were attracted to her angelic face. She bowed humbly to all and sat beside her father. Her father asked her affectionately – "Dear Savitri, how was your trip through the country? Could you find a suitable prince to wed you?"

The whole court was anxious to hear her answer. As everyone wished a bright future for their most beautiful and talented princess. The king had sent her along with the senior ministers to choose a husband worthy of her. She had come back after a tour of one month.

Savitri replied modestly – "Yes Father, I have chosen Satayavan, son of Dumatsen ,the exiled King of Shalava State."

"Satayavan" – the name echoed in the air. Narada Rishi, present there, was startled to hear it. His face looked worried. The king looked at him with anxiety.

Narada replied – "Maharaj, your daughter has chosen the best prince for her. He is bright like the Sun, brave like God Inder, wise like Brishapati and handsome like God Moon. But all his qualities suffer from one defect just like an eclipse on the Moon."

The king asked worriedly – "And what is that Rishivar?"

"Maharaj, Satayavan is short-lived."

"Short-lived?" the word fell like thunderbolt in the court.

"Yes, Maharaj, he has taken a vow to renounce everything in the world and become a monk after one year. Therefore your talented daughter should not choose a life of widowhood." Narada advised the King.

His prediction filled everyone's heart with sorrow for the princess. The King was shocked to tears for her only daughter's dark future. He held her hands and said, "Dear daughter, I cannot let this happen to you. Go back and choose another prince who is worthy for you."

Savitri sat calm and quiet. There was no trace of anxiety on her pretty face.

King said again – "Savitri, Bharat has so many talented princes who are far superior to Satayavan. How can Satayavan be worthy for you who is devoid of his State and living in exile like a coward? And the worst part is that he is going to renounce the world and become a monk. Think over it wisely, Savitri ! Your precious life is not meant to be thrown away."

Savitri had now regained her poise. Sweetly smiling she replied - "Father, your worry is born out of your deep love for me. But there is no cause for this. With the consent of your able ministers, I have chosen Satayavan as my future husband. He is endowed with all the qualities except one. For that, please have faith in me I will take care of that. So you need not worry for my future. With your blessing, I will make it bright."

Her words spoke of the strength of her character. All sat mesmerised to hear her decision but father's heart was not fully relieved. He anxiously looked towards Rishi Narada.

Then Narada Rishi said – "Maharaj, I am fully convinced with Savitri's ideas. She is capable to accomplish what she has decided. I advise you to have faith in her and let her fulfil her vow to wed Satyavan."

The King submitted to Narada's advice and her daughter's decision. On an auspicious day, he travelled to Dumatsen's ashram in the forest along with her daughter and dowry. Even Dumatsen tried to dissuade Savitri to marry his son due to his resolve to renounce. But Savitri stood firm like a rock on her vow to wed only Satayavan. So they were married by the priest and after giving their blessings the parents took their leave.

After the marriage, Savitri gave away her royal dresses and jewellery to the women of neighbourhood. She put on the simple dress like an ordinary woman and took over the duties of a daughter-in-law. Her old father-in-law and mother-in-law had doubts as to how the princess would take to this hard life of ashrama. But Savitri embraced their way of life with such art and humility that all loved her dearly. But whenever Satayavan looked at her beautiful wife busy in mundane work at home, his heart was pained. After thinking of his resolve to renounce, he felt worried for her future.

Savitri did not let anyone know what went on in her mind. Sometimes sitting alone, her eyes were filled with tears. She felt terribly alone and depressed thinking of her future. Her heart revolted to see her husband leading the life of a coward. A question always rang in her ears – "When will he realise his real self of a Kshatriya? When will he manifest his manhood? What will happen after one year when...?" And she could not think further.

But time never stops. At last the day dawned when Satayavan was to renounce the world. Everyone knew this. So all looked worried for them. Savitri, too, looked grave but her gravity was not the result of sadness but of strength.

When Satayavan started to go to the forest for his usual daily routine of bringing firewood for the kitchen, Savitri asked her mother-in-law to permit her to accompany him. She was permitted to go. Both started for the forest. After marriage, it was the first time that they were alone. Both felt a new sensation of love. They held each-other's hands and went talking and laughing like the newly-weds.

They worked hard for the whole day. They ate their food together. As the day advanced, Satayavan felt tired and lay to rest on Savitri's knees. Savitri looked at his face. It was calm and quiet while her own face showed the storm raging in her heart.

"Why do you look so perturbed today Savitri? Look at the

setting sun! How gentle and peaceful it is!" Satayavan said.

Hearing his words, Savitri lost her patience for the first time. She spoke strongly – "Swami, the sun becomes cool and peaceful after burning brightly for the whole day."

The fire in her voice surprised him. Her words spoke of her heart's anguish. Her flushed face was new to him. Her soft eyes had turned into pools of fire.

He asked - "Savitri, you seem to be very disturbed by my resolve of renunciation."

Savitri was quick to reply – "Not I alone, even your parents are disturbed. The loss of their kingdom did not pain them so much as this loss of their only son. They had expected you to become their support in old age. They had never thought that they would lose their only son and be left helpless, penniless, alone in this world of wilderness. Today the people of your State, too, would lose all hopes of freedom. Your enemy would rejoice at their victory without a battle. And this is all due to your resolve for renunciation. Today let me ask you for the first time: What will you gain after leaving your wife a widow with no son or wealth and your parents helpless? This renunciation is, in fact, running away from your duties. Why don't you realise your real self? You have forgotten that you are a Kshatriya King who is responsible for the life and prosperity of his people. Your hands have been destined to hold a sword and a Royal sceptre. These are not meant to hold a monk's begging bowl. These are made to provide for your people who look towards you as their Saviour. How can you turn your back to your destiny and renounce like a coward? This body of a warrior is meant to adorn arms to fight the enemy and win back your kingdom."

Savitri went on saying and Satayavan listening. Each word hit him like thunderbolt. Her stirring words ignited the fire out of his sleeping spring of life. He felt the courage and conviction of her words. It was as if a veil had been lifted away from his eyes and he saw everything in broad day light. He saw his duties and his cowardice too. There was no moment to lose now. He had already lost much time.

He got up with a start. He looked towards her brave wife and pressed her hands in gratitude. Now he strode strongly towards home holding Savitri's hands. It was a new Satayavan now as if it was his re-birth.

He plunged into work day and night. He gathered men and arms. After preparing his men to fight a battle, he fought a decisive battle with the enemy and won back his kingdom. This gave a new lease of life to his blind old father and mother. Savitri had fulfilled her vow to enliven her husband into a new life. Now she lived a life of bliss with her sons.

□

Daughter of the Himalayas

The snow-clad peaks of the Himalayas encircled that secluded corner of the forest where stood a small hut. There lived a fair maiden whose divine beauty and indomitable courage seemed to have sprung from those mountains.

She was Parvati – the only daughter of the King of the mountain-state. She had come to this place to pray and do penance to achieve her heart's desire.

And her heart's desire was to be the wife of Lord Shiva whom she loved with her whole heart and soul. She loved him when she had opened her eyes in this world. Her friends made fun of her and asked her, "How could one love a person without seeing or knowing him?" But Parvati's reply was – "I need not see his photo as he is in my heart. I see him always with me." She used to sit alone and think of him with eyes closed. Everyone called her 'Shiva-Diwani' (mad after Shiva).

As she grew up, her father asked from Dev Rishi Narada – "Dev Rishi, you roam about the whole universe and possess heavenly knowledge. Tell me, whether my daughter's love for Lord Shiva would be successful?"

Dev Rishi's reply was – "No doubt, it is difficult to persuade a celibate like Shivji for this bond of marriage. One who has no home or hearth, who never cares for his own food or shelter, how can he be made ready to take the responsibility of a life partner?"

"Then, what would become of my daughter?" the king asked anxiously because he knew her daughter's resolve was either to wed Shivji or embrace death. Narada said, "Maharaj, there's only one path that leads to Shivji and that is of hard penance. The girl has to be very patient, self-controlled, simple, pure and non-desirous of worldly wealth. Shivji cannot be won by wealth or beauty." Parvati listened to his words from behind the door.

She took these words to her heart and began living like that. Though a princess, she discarded royal dress and jewellery and wore a simple dress. She was already well-versed in all the great epics and Puranas. Now she started living like a student in an Ashram. Her mother felt sad to see her darling daughter living in this way. One day she got the shock of her life when Parvati asked mother to permit her to go to the forest for doing penance.

Embracing her she wailed, "Oh, dear, how can I permit you to live in a secluded hut in the forest? How would you bear the cold and heat in the wilderness? No, I will never permit you."

But Parvati was adamant in her resolve. So mother had to give her permission. Now Parvati had been living in this hut with her friend for many months.

One evening, a young monk visited them. Parvati was busy in prayers. Her friend welcomed the monk. He asked her – "Why is your friend leading such a hard life and doing penance?"

She replied – "My friend is doing this to get Shivji as her husband."

On hearing these words, the monk burst into a laughter and said – "Devi, advise your friend to give up such a foolish effort. That snake-wearing half-clad yogi is no match for this beautiful princess. How will he sustain a wife who has no home of his own? That pauper is not worthy of such a gem! This would mean throwing a flower in the mud or trampling a gem under the feet."

"Stop now, Tapasavi," Parvati left her seat and shouted at the monk in fury. "I do not want to listen to a single word against my Shivji. If you have no sense to know his greatness, please do not criticise him. It is like spitting on the moon." And she went away hiding her tears of remorse.

Tapasavi smiled mysteriously and went his way. After a while the king came there and embracing his daughter said joyously – "Parvati, your penance has borne fruits. Now, let us go home." Parvati could not ask the details out of modesty. But when she came to know later that the visitor was no other than her own beloved Shivji who had come to give a last test to his life-partner, she was beside herself with pleasure.

When after her wedding the princess reached her own home on the highest peak of Kailash Parvat, her life's dream was realised. She was created to be the Goddess of Shakti and wife of Kailash-King Shivji. Her only wealth was her love. It was the power of love that made her invincible when she fought the Demons in later life. She was the proud mother of Kartikaya – the Commander of Devta's Army and Ganesha – the God of Learning.

□□□